A TANGLED WEB

Short Stories

EDITED BY
Christine Lindop
Alison Sykes-McNulty

SERIES ADVISERS
H. G. Widdowson
Jennifer Bassett

OXFORD UNIVERSITY PRESS
2005

OXFORD
UNIVERSITY PRESS

Great Clarendon Street, Oxford OX2 6DP

Oxford University Press is a department of the University of Oxford.
It furthers the University's objective of excellence in research, scholarship,
and education by publishing worldwide in

Oxford New York

Auckland Cape Town Dar es Salaam Hong Kong Karachi
Kuala Lumpur Madrid Melbourne Mexico City Nairobi
New Delhi Shanghai Taipei Toronto

With offices in

Argentina Austria Brazil Chile Czech Republic France Greece
Guatemala Hungary Italy Japan Poland Portugal Singapore
South Korea Switzerland Thailand Turkey Ukraine Vietnam

OXFORD and OXFORD ENGLISH are registered trade marks of
Oxford University Press in the UK and in certain other countries

ISBN : 978 0 19 422814 5

Printed in China

OXFORD BOOKWORMS
～ COLLECTION ～

FOREWORD

Texts of all kinds, including literary texts, are used as data for language teaching. They are designed or adapted and pressed into service to exemplify the language and provide practice in reading. These are commendable pedagogic purposes. They are not, however, what authors or readers of texts usually have in mind. The reason we read something is because we feel the writer has something of interest or significance to say and we only attend to the language to the extent that it helps us to understand what that might be. An important part of language learning is knowing how to adopt this normal reader role, how to use language to achieve meanings of significance to us, and so make texts our own.

The purpose of the *Oxford Bookworms Collection* is to encourage students of English to adopt this role. It offers samples of English language fiction, unabridged and unsimplified, which have been selected and presented to induce enjoyment, and to develop a sensitivity to the language through an appreciation of the literature. The intention is to stimulate students to find in fiction what Jane Austen found: 'the most thorough knowledge of human nature, the happiest delineation of its varieties, the liveliest effusions of wit and humour . . . conveyed to the world in the best chosen language.' *(Northanger Abbey)*

H. G. Widdowson
Series Adviser

Oxford Bookworms
~ Collection ~

None of the texts has been abridged or simplified in any way, but each volume contains notes and questions to help students in their understanding and appreciation.

Before each story
- a short biographical note on the author
- an introduction to the theme and characters of the story

After each story
- NOTES

  Some words and phrases in the texts are marked with an asterisk*, and explanations for these are given in the notes. The expressions selected are usually cultural references or archaic and dialect words unlikely to be found in dictionaries. Other difficult words are not explained. This is because to do so might be to focus attention too much on the analysis of particular meanings, and to disrupt the natural reading process. Students should be encouraged by their engagement with the story to infer general and relevant meaning from context.

- DISCUSSION

  These are questions on the story's theme and characters, designed to stimulate class discussion or to encourage the individual reader to think about the story from different points of view.

- LANGUAGE FOCUS

  Some of these questions and tasks direct the reader's attention to particular features of language use or style; others focus on specific meanings and their significance in the story.

- ACTIVITIES

  These are suggestions for creative writing activities, to encourage readers to explore or develop the themes of the story in various imaginative ways.

- QUESTIONS FOR DISCUSSION OR WRITING

  These are questions (sometimes under the heading 'Ideas for Comparison Activities') with ideas for discussion or writing which compare and contrast a number of stories in the volume.

CURRENT TITLES

From the Cradle to the Grave   The Eye of Childhood
Crime Never Pays   And All for Love . . .
A Window on the Universe   A Tangled Web

A TANGLED WEB

O what a tangled web we weave,
When first we practise to deceive.
SIR WALTER SCOTT

Deception comes in many shapes and sizes. There is the small white lie, where the intention is to be kind, to avoid hurting someone's feelings with the truth. At the other end of the scale there are the big deceptions: lies told to escape punishment for wrongdoing, lies told to defraud, to cheat, to bear false witness. Another kind of deception is allowing someone else to continue with a false assumption, when we could put them right with a word. But do we always need or want to know the truth? 'Where ignorance is bliss, 'tis folly to be wise,' wrote the poet Thomas Gray.

A silence, a failure to act, a small untruth, a bold and naked lie . . . In these stories we see how quickly a first step on this path can lead to a tangled web, with unforeseen and often unwelcome results. But by then it is usually too late to turn back. The stone has been thrown into the water, the ripples are spreading out, and there is nothing we can do about it.

We begin with an old lie, a deception that husbands and wives have practised ever since marriage was invented, but here it has a rather different modern twist . . .

OXFORD BOOKWORMS COLLECTION

Acknowledgements

The editors and publishers are grateful for permission to use the following copyright material:

'Telling Stories' by MAEVE BINCHY, from *Telling Stories* published by Coronet 1992. Copyright © Maeve Binchy 1992. Reprinted by permission of Christine Green Authors' Agent.

'Edna, Back from America' by CLARE BOYLAN, taken from her collection, *That Bad Woman*, published by Abacus. Copyright © 1994 by Clare Boylan. Reproduced by permission of the author c/o Rogers, Coleridge & White Ltd., 20 Powis Mews, London W11 1JN.

'Marionettes, Inc.' from *The Illustrated Man* by RAY BRADBURY. Reprinted by permission of Abner Stein.

'Taste' from *Someone Like You* by ROALD DAHL, published by Michael Joseph Ltd and Penguin Books Ltd. Reprinted by permission of David Higham Associates.

'Sharp Practice' from *No Comebacks* by FREDERICK FORSYTH, published by Hutchinson, 1982. Used by permission of The Random House Group Limited.

'Mr Know-All' from *The Complete Short Stories* by W. SOMERSET MAUGHAM, first published by William Heinemann Ltd 1951. Reprinted by permission of A. P. Watt Ltd on behalf of The Royal Literary Fund.

'The Coward' from *Miguel Street* by V. S. NAIPAUL, published by Penguin 1971. Copyright © 1959 V. S. Naipaul. Reprinted by permission of Gillon Aitken Associates.

'Neighbours' from *The London Embassy* by PAUL THEROUX, published by Hamish Hamilton 1982. Copyright © Paul Theroux 1982. Reprinted by permission of Penguin Books Ltd.

'The Hero' by JOANNA TROLLOPE from *Telling Stories Volume 4*, published by Hodder & Stoughton 1995. Copyright © Joanna Trollope 1994. Reprinted by permission of the Peters Fraser & Dunlop Group Ltd.

Contents

MARIONETTES, INC.

THE AUTHOR

Ray Bradbury was born in 1920 in Illinois, USA, and became a full-time writer in 1943. His reputation as a leading writer of science fiction was established with *The Martian Chronicles*, a series of stories about attempts by humans to colonize Mars. Another of his well-known works is the novel *Fahrenheit 451* (1953), which is set in a totalitarian future when books are burned because ideas are dangerous. This was made into a film in 1966 by François Truffaut. Among Bradbury's many collections of short stories are *The Illustrated Man*, *The Golden Apples of the Sun*, and *The Day It Rained Forever*.

THE STORY

Is there a dream, a wish, waiting unfulfilled somewhere in the back of your mind? Are there days when you would rather tiptoe away from your job, your relationships, your responsibilities, and do just what you please? What if you could convince everyone that life was going on as usual, while in reality you were elsewhere pursuing your dream?

Braling – quiet, dependable, serious Braling – thinks that he has found the way to do just this. After ten years in a loveless marriage, he is only days away from realizing a long-cherished dream. So confident is he that his plan will succeed that he decides to let his friend Smith in on the secret. After the first shock, Smith is deeply impressed and rather envious . . .

MARIONETTES, INC.

They walked slowly down the street at about ten in the evening, talking calmly. They were both about thirty-five, both eminently sober.

'But why so early?' said Smith.

'Because,' said Braling.

'Your first night out in years and you go home at ten o'clock.'

'Nerves, I suppose.'

'What I wonder is how you ever managed it. I've been trying to get you out for ten years for a quiet drink. And now, on the one night, you insist on turning in early.'

'Mustn't crowd my luck*,' said Braling.

'What did you do, put sleeping powder in your wife's coffee?'

'No, that would be unethical. You'll see soon enough.'

They turned a corner. 'Honestly, Braling, I hate to say this, but, you *have* been patient with her. You may not admit it to me, but marriage has been awful for you, hasn't it?'

'I wouldn't say that.'

'It's got around, anyway, here and there, how she got you to marry her. That time back in 1979 when you were going to Rio—'

'Dear Rio. I never *did* see it after all my plans.'

'And how she tore her clothes and rumpled her hair and threatened to call the police unless you married her.'

'She always was nervous, Smith, understand.'

'It was more than unfair. You didn't love her. You told her as much, didn't you?'

'I recall that I was quite firm on the subject.'

'But you married her anyhow.'

'I had my business to think of, as well as my mother and father. A thing like that would have killed them.'

'And it's been ten years.'

'Yes,' said Braling, his grey eyes steady. 'But I think perhaps it might change now. I think what I've waited for has come about. Look here.'

He drew forth a long blue ticket.

'Why, it's a ticket for Rio on the Thursday rocket!'

'Yes, I'm finally going to make it.'

'But how wonderful! You *do* deserve it! But won't *she* object? Cause trouble?'

Braling smiled nervously. 'She won't know I'm gone. I'll be back in a month and no one the wiser, except you.'

Smith sighed. 'I wish I were going with you.'

'Poor Smith, *your* marriage hasn't exactly been roses, has it?'

'Not exactly, married to a woman who overdoes it. I mean, after all, when you've been married ten years, you don't expect a woman to sit on your lap for two hours every evening, call you at work twelve times a day and talk baby talk. And it seems to me that in the last month she's gotten worse. I wonder if perhaps she isn't just a little simple-minded?'

'Ah, Smith, always the conservative. Well, here's my house. Now, would you like to know my secret? How I made it out this evening?'

'Will you really tell?'

'Look up there!' said Braling.

They both stared up through the dark air.

In the window above them, on the second floor, a shade was raised. A man about thirty-five years old, with a touch of grey at either temple, sad grey eyes, and a small thin moustache looked down at them.

'Why, that's *you*!' cried Smith.

'Sh-h-h, not so loud!' Braling waved upward. The man in the window gestured significantly and vanished.

'I must be insane,' said Smith.

'Hold on a moment.'

They waited.

The street door of the apartment opened and the tall spare gentleman with the moustache and the grieved eyes came out to meet them.

'Hello, Braling,' he said.

'Hello, Braling,' said Braling.

They were identical.

Smith stared. 'Is this your twin brother? I never knew—'

'No, no,' said Braling quietly. 'Bend close. Put your ear to Braling Two's chest.'

Smith hesitated and then leaned forward to place his head against the uncomplaining ribs.

Tick-tick-tick-tick-tick-tick-tick-tick.

'Oh, no! It can't be!'

'It is.'

'Let me listen again.'

Tick-tick-tick-tick-tick-tick-tick-tick.

Smith staggered back and fluttered his eyelids, appalled. He reached out and touched the warm hands and the cheeks of the thing.

'Where'd you get him?'

'Isn't he excellently fashioned?'

'Incredible. Where?'

'Give the man your card, Braling Two.'

Braling Two did a magic trick and produced a white card:

MARIONETTES, INC.

Duplicate self or friends; new humanoid plastic 1990 models, guaranteed against all physical wear. From $7,600 to our $15,000 de luxe model.

'No,' said Smith.

'Yes,' said Braling.

'Naturally,' said Braling Two.

'How long has this gone on?'

'I've had him for a month. I keep him in the cellar in a toolbox. My wife never goes downstairs, and I have the only lock and key to that box. Tonight I said I wished to take a walk to buy a cigar. I went down to the cellar and took Braling Two out of his box and sent him back up to sit with my wife while I came on out to see you, Smith.'

'Wonderful! He even *smells* like you: Bond Street* and Melachrinos*!'

'It may be splitting hairs, but I think it highly ethical. After all, what my wife wants most of all is *me*. This marionette *is* me to the hairiest detail. I've been home all evening. I shall be home with her for the next month. In the meantime another gentleman will be in Rio after ten years of waiting. When I return from Rio, Braling Two here will go back in his box.'

Smith thought that over a minute or two. 'Will he walk around without sustenance for a month?' he finally asked.

'For six months if necessary. And he's built to do everything – eat, sleep, perspire – everything, natural as natural is. You'll take good care of my wife, won't you, Braling Two?'

'Your wife is rather nice,' said Braling Two. 'I've grown rather fond of her.'

Smith was beginning to tremble. 'How long has Marionettes, Inc., been in business?'

'Secretly, for two years.'

'Could I – I mean, is there a possibility—' Smith took his friend's elbow earnestly. 'Can you tell me where I can get one, a robot, a marionette, for myself? You *will* give me the address, won't you?'

'Here you are.'

Smith took the card and turned it round and round. 'Thank you,' he said. 'You don't know what this means. Just a little respite. A night or so, once a month even. My wife loves me so much she can't bear to have me gone an hour. I love her dearly, you know, but remember the old poem: "Love will fly if held too lightly, love will die if held too tightly." I just want her to relax her grip a little bit.'

'You're lucky, at least, that your wife loves you. Hate's my problem. Not so easy.'

'Oh, Nettie loves me madly. It will be my task to make her love me comfortably.'

'Good luck to you, Smith. Do drop around while I'm in Rio. It will seem strange, if you suddenly stop calling by, to my wife. You're to treat Braling Two here, just like me.'

'Right! Good-bye. And thank you.'

Smith went smiling down the street. Braling and Braling Two turned and walked into the apartment hall.

On the crosstown bus Smith whistled softly, turning the white card in his fingers:

Clients must be pledged to secrecy, for while an act is pending in Congress* to legalize Marionettes, Inc., it is still a felony, if caught, to use one.

'Well,' said Smith.

Clients must have a mould made of their body and a colour index check of their eyes, lips, hair, skin, etc. Clients must expect to wait for two months until their model is finished.

Not so long, thought Smith. Two months from now my ribs will have a chance to mend from the crushing they've taken. Two months from now my hand will heal from being so constantly held. Two months from now my bruised underlip will begin to reshape itself. I don't mean to sound *ungrateful* . . . He flipped the card over.

> Marionettes, Inc., is two years old and has a fine record of satisfied customers behind it. Our motto is 'No Strings Attached'. Address: 43 South Wesley Drive.

The bus pulled to his stop; he alighted, and while humming up the stairs he thought, Nettie and I have fifteen thousand in our joint bank account. I'll just slip eight thousand out as a business venture, you might say. The marionette will probably pay back my money, with interest, in many ways. Nettie needn't know. He unlocked the door and in a minute was in the bedroom. There lay Nettie, pale, huge, and piously asleep.

'Dear Nettie.' He was almost overwhelmed with remorse at her innocent face there in the semi-darkness. 'If you were awake you would smother me with kisses and coo in my ear. Really, you make me feel like a criminal. You have been such a good, loving wife. Sometimes it is impossible for me to believe you married me instead of that Bud Chapman you once liked. It seems that in the last month you have loved me more wildly than *ever* before.'

Tears came to his eyes. Suddenly, he wished to kiss her, confess his love, tear up the card, forget the whole business. But as he moved to do this, his hand ached and his ribs cracked and groaned. He stopped, with a pained look in his eyes, and turned away. He moved out into the hall and through the dark rooms. Humming, he opened the kidney desk* in the library and filched the bankbook. 'Just take eight thousand dollars is all,' he said. 'No more than that.' He stopped. 'Wait a minute.'

He rechecked the bankbook frantically. 'Hold on here!' he cried. 'Ten thousand dollars is missing!' He leaped up. 'There's only five thousand left! What's she done? What's Nettie done with it? More hats, more clothes, more perfume! Oh, wait – I know! She bought that little house on the Hudson she's been talking about for months, without so much as a by your leave!'

He stormed into the bedroom, righteous and indignant. What did she mean, taking their money like this? He bent over her. 'Nettie!' he shouted. 'Nettie, wake up!'

She did not stir. 'What've you done with my money!' he bellowed.

She stirred fitfully. The light from the street flushed over her beautiful cheeks.

There was something about her. His heart throbbed violently. His tongue dried. He shivered. His knees suddenly turned to water. He collapsed. 'Nettie, Nettie!' he cried. 'What've you done with my money!'

And then, the horrid thought. And then the terror and the loneliness engulfed him. And then the fever and disillusionment. For, without desiring to do so, he bent forward and yet forward again until his fevered ear was resting firmly and irrevocably upon her round pink bosom. 'Nettie!' he cried.

Tick-tick-tick-tick-tick-tick-tick-tick-tick-tick-tick.

As Smith walked away down the avenue in the night, Braling and Braling Two turned in at the door to the apartment. 'I'm glad he'll be happy too,' said Braling.

'Yes,' said Braling Two abstractedly.

'Well, it's the cellar box for you, B-Two.' Braling guided the other creature's elbow down the stairs to the cellar.

'That's what I want to talk to you about,' said Braling Two, as they reached the concrete floor and walked across it. 'The cellar. I don't like it. I don't like that toolbox.'

'I'll try and fix up something more comfortable.'

'Marionettes are made to move, not lie still. How would you like to lie in a box most of the time?'

'Well—'

'You wouldn't like it all. I keep running. There's no way to shut me off. I'm perfectly alive and I have feelings.'

'It'll only be a few days now. I'll be off to Rio and you won't have to stay in the box. You can live upstairs.'

Braling Two gestured irritably. 'And when you come back from having a good time, back in the box I go.'

Braling said, 'They didn't tell me at the marionette shop that I'd get a difficult specimen.'

'There's a lot they don't know about us,' said Braling Two. 'We're pretty new. And we're sensitive. I hate the idea of you going off and laughing and lying in the sun in Rio while we're stuck here in the cold.'

'But I've wanted that trip all my life,' said Braling quietly.

He squinted his eyes and could see the sea and the mountains and the yellow sand. The sound of the waves was good to his inward mind. The sun was fine on his bared shoulders. The wine was most excellent.

'*I'll* never get to go to Rio,' said the other man. 'Have you thought of that?'

'No, I—'

'And another thing. Your wife.'

'What about her?' asked Braling, beginning to edge toward the door.

'I've grown quite fond of her.'

'I'm glad you're enjoying your employment.' Braling licked his lips nervously.

'I'm afraid you don't understand. I think – I'm in love with her.'

Braling took another step and froze. 'You're *what*?'

'And I've been thinking,' said Braling Two, 'how nice it is in Rio and how I'll never get there, and I've thought about your wife and – I think we could be very happy.'

'Th-that's nice.' Braling strolled as casually as he could to the cellar door. 'You won't mind waiting a moment, will you? I have to make a phone call.'

'To whom?' Braling Two frowned.

'No one important.'

'To Marionettes, Incorporated? To tell them to come get me?'

'No, no – nothing like that!' He tried to rush out the door.

A metal-firm grip seized his wrists. 'Don't run!'

'Take your hands off!'

'No.'

'Did my wife put you up to this?'

'No.'

'Did she guess? Did she talk to you? Does she know? Is *that* it?' He screamed. A hand clapped over his mouth.

'You'll never know, will you?' Braling Two smiled delicately. 'You'll never know.'

Braling struggled. 'She *must* have guessed; she *must* have affected you!'

Braling Two said, 'I'm going to put you in the box, lock it, and lose the key. Then I'll buy another Rio ticket for your wife.'

'Now, now, wait a minute. Hold on. Don't be rash. Let's talk this over!'

'Good-bye, Braling.'

Braling stiffened. 'What do you mean, "good-bye"?'

Ten minutes later Mrs. Braling awoke. She put her hand to her cheek. Someone had just kissed it. She shivered and looked up. 'Why – you haven't done that in years,' she murmured.

'We'll see what we can do about that,' someone said.

NOTES

crowd my luck (p10)
   put my good luck at risk by being over-confident
Bond Street (p13)
   a brand of tobacco
Melachrinos (p13)
   a brand of cigarettes
an act is pending in Congress (p14)
   a law is in the process of being passed by the body that makes laws
   for the United States of America
kidney desk (p15)
   a desk with curved ends, in the shape of a kidney

DISCUSSION

1 How far are the feelings Smith and Braling have about their marriages
   the same and how far are they different? How much sympathy do you
   have for them? Or for their wives?

2 Does Braling treat Braling 2 well? Should he do so? Does he deserve the
   treatment he gets from Braling 2?

3 Marionettes Inc. is still not legalized. What objections do you think
   might be raised to legalizing it? Do you think there are circumstances
   which would justify the use of such marionettes?

4 What evidence is there in the story that it is set in the future?

LANGUAGE FOCUS

1 Rephrase these expressions from the story in your own words.

   'your marriage hasn't exactly been roses, has it?' (p11)
   'It may be splitting hairs' (p13)
   'natural as natural is' (p13)
   without so much as a by your leave (p16)
   His knees suddenly turned to water (p16)
   'Did my wife put you up to this?' (p18)

2 *'And it seems to me that in the last month she's gotten worse. I
   wonder if perhaps she isn't just a little simple-minded?'* (p11)
   Can you explain why Smith should get this impression of his wife?

3 *I'll just slip eight thousand out as a business venture . . . Nettie*
   needn't know. (p15) *What did she mean, taking their money like this?*
   (p16)
   Compare these two statements of Smith's. What do they reveal about
   his attitudes towards his wife and money?

4 *And then, the horrid thought. And then the terror and the loneliness*
   engulfed him. And then the fever and disillusionment. (p16)
   Can you explain this sequence of reactions that Smith goes through?
   What is the horrid thought, and what causes each of the feelings that
   follow?

5 *'We'll see what we can do about that,' someone said.* (p18)
   What is the effect of using 'someone' here, rather than a name?

ACTIVITIES

1 What do you suppose Mrs Smith has done? Where has she gone? What
   do you think has made her take this step? Write a farewell note from
   her to her husband, explaining her plans and her reasons for them.

2 How might this story continue? Does Mrs Braling become suspicious
   of her husband's attentions, or does she accept them without asking
   questions? What does Smith do about the awful situation he finds
   himself in? Write a paragraph or two to show how you think things
   proceed.

3 Suppose that Congress does legalize the use of marionettes in this way.
   What restrictions might they place on their use? Should it be legal, for
   example, for a husband to replace himself without his wife's
   knowledge? When could you legally duplicate a friend? Write a list of
   recommendations for the restrictions and conditions that Congress
   might incorporate into their law.

4 Do you think *Marionettes, Inc.* is a good title for this story? Why, or
   why not? What other titles can you think of that would arouse the
   reader's interest without giving away the ending?

TASTE

THE AUTHOR

Roald Dahl was born in Wales in 1916 of Norwegian parents. He served as a fighter pilot in World War II, and his first volume of short stories, *Over to You*, was based on his wartime experiences. Other collections are *Kiss Kiss, Someone Like You, Switch Bitch*, and *Further Tales of the Unexpected;* they have been translated into many languages and are bestsellers all over the world. His storytelling is bizarre, alarming, and disturbing, often with a touch of black humour and a nasty sting in the tail. His stories for children, such as *Charlie and the Chocolate Factory*, are also very popular. He died in 1990.

THE STORY

Wine 'maketh glad the heart of man', says the Bible, and indeed for many people a good bottle of wine is one of the great pleasures of life. Add good company, excellent food, and pleasant surroundings, and you have all the requirements for a perfectly delightful evening.

Or do you? In Mike Schofield's house the table is set and the aroma of dinner fills the air, but under the surface an unpleasant tension is beginning to grow and Mike is about to go into battle with the famous gourmet Richard Pratt over a bottle of wine . . .

TASTE

There were six of us to dinner that night at Mike Schofield's house in London: Mike and his wife and daughter, my wife and I, and a man called Richard Pratt.

Richard Pratt was a famous gourmet. He was president of a small society known as the Epicures, and each month he circulated privately to its members a pamphlet on food and wines. He organized dinners where sumptuous dishes and rare wines were served. He refused to smoke for fear of harming his palate, and when discussing wine, he had a curious, rather droll habit of referring to it as though it were a living being. 'A prudent wine,' he would say, 'rather diffident and evasive, but quite prudent.' Or, 'A good-humoured wine, benevolent and cheerful – slightly obscene, perhaps, but none the less good-humoured.'

I had been to dinner at Mike's twice before when Richard Pratt was there, and on each occasion Mike and his wife had gone out of their way to produce a special meal for the famous gourmet. And this one, clearly, was to be no exception. The moment we entered the dining-room, I could see that the table was laid for a feast. The tall candles, the yellow roses, the quantity of shining silver, the three wineglasses to each person, and above all, the faint scent of roasting meat from the kitchen brought the first warm oozings of saliva to my mouth.

As we sat down, I remembered that on both Richard Pratt's previous visits Mike had played a little betting game with him over the claret, challenging him to name its breed and its vintage. Pratt had replied that that should not be too difficult provided it was one of the great years. Mike had then bet him a case of the wine in question that he could not do it. Pratt had accepted, and had won both times. Tonight I felt sure that the little game would be played over again, for Mike was quite willing to lose the bet in order to prove that his wine was good enough to be recognized, and Pratt, for his part, seemed to take a grave, restrained pleasure in displaying his knowledge.

The meal began with a plate of whitebait, fried very crisp in butter, and to go with it there was a Moselle. Mike got up and poured the wine himself, and when he sat down again, I could see that he was watching Richard Pratt. He had set the bottle in front of me so that I could read the label. It said, 'Geierslay Ohligsberg, 1945'. He leaned over and whispered to me that Geierslay was a tiny village in the Moselle, almost unknown outside Germany. He said that this wine we were drinking was something unusual, that the output of the vineyard was so small that it was almost impossible for a stranger to get any of it. He had visited Geierslay personally the previous summer in order to obtain the few dozen bottles that they had finally allowed him to have.

'I doubt whether anyone else in the country has any of it at the moment,' he said. I saw him glance again at Richard Pratt. 'Great thing about Moselle,' he continued, raising his voice, 'it's the perfect wine to serve before a claret. A lot of people serve a Rhine wine instead, but that's because they don't know any better. A Rhine wine will kill a delicate claret, you know that? It's barbaric to serve a Rhine before a claret. But a Moselle – ah! – a Moselle is exactly right.'

Mike Schofield was an amiable, middle-aged man. But he was a stockbroker. To be precise, he was a jobber* in the stock market, and like a number of his kind, he seemed to be somewhat embarrassed, almost ashamed to find that he had made so much money with so slight a talent. In his heart he knew that he was not really much more than a bookmaker – an unctuous, infinitely respectable, secretly unscrupulous bookmaker – and he knew that his friends knew it, too. So he was seeking now to become a man of culture, to cultivate a literary and aesthetic taste, to collect paintings, music, books, and all the rest of it. His little sermon about Rhine wine and Moselle was a part of this thing, this culture that he sought.

'A charming little wine, don't you think?' he said. He was still watching Richard Pratt. I could see him give a rapid furtive glance down the table each time he dropped his head to take a mouthful of whitebait. I could almost feel him waiting for the moment when Pratt would take his first sip, and look up from his glass with a smile of pleasure, of astonishment, perhaps even of wonder, and then there would be a discussion and Mike would tell him about the village of Geierslay.

But Richard Pratt did not taste his wine. He was completely engrossed in conversation with Mike's eighteen-year-old daughter, Louise. He was half turned towards her, smiling at her, telling her, so far as I could gather, some story about a chef in a Paris restaurant. As he spoke, he leaned closer and closer to her, seeming in his eagerness almost to impinge upon her, and the poor girl leaned as far as she could away from him, nodding politely, rather desperately, and looking not at his face but at the topmost button of his dinner jacket.

We finished our fish, and the maid came round removing the plates. When she came to Pratt, she saw that he had not yet touched his food, so she hesitated, and Pratt noticed her. He waved her away, broke off his conversation, and quickly began to eat, popping the little crisp brown fish quickly into his mouth with rapid jabbing movements of his fork. Then, when he had finished, he reached for his glass, and in two short swallows he tipped the wine down his throat and turned immediately to resume his conversation with Louise Schofield.

Mike saw it all. I was conscious of him sitting there, very still, containing himself, looking at his guest. His round jovial face seemed to loosen slightly and to sag, but he contained himself and was still and said nothing.

Soon the maid came forward with the second course. This was a large roast of beef. She placed it on the table in front of Mike who stood up and carved it, cutting the slices very thin, laying them gently on the plates for the maid to take around. When he had served everyone, including himself, he put down the carving knife and leaned forward with both hands on the edge of the table.

'Now,' he said, speaking to all of us but looking at Richard Pratt. 'Now for the claret. I must go and fetch the claret, if you'll excuse me.'

'You go and fetch it, Mike?' I said. 'Where is it?'

'In my study, with the cork out – breathing.'

'Why the study?'

'Acquiring room temperature, of course. It's been there twenty-four hours.'

'But why the study?'

'It's the best place in the house. Richard helped me choose it last time he was here.'

At the sound of his name, Pratt looked round.

'That's right, isn't it?' Mike said.

'Yes,' Pratt answered, nodding gravely. 'That's right.'

'On top of the green filing cabinet in my study,' Mike said. 'That's the place we chose. A good draught-free spot in a room with an even temperature. Excuse me now, will you, while I fetch it.'

The thought of another wine to play with had restored his humour, and he hurried out of the door, to return a minute later more slowly, walking softly, holding in both hands a wine basket in which a dark bottle lay. The label was out of sight, facing downwards. 'Now! he cried as he came towards the table. 'What about this one, Richard? You'll never name this one!'

Richard Pratt turned slowly and looked up at Mike, then his
eyes travelled down to the bottle nestling in its small wicker
basket, and he raised his eyebrows, a slight, supercilious arching of
the brows, and with it a pushing outward of the wet lower lip,
suddenly imperious and ugly.

'You'll never get it,' Mike said. 'Not in a hundred years.'

'A claret?' Richard Pratt asked, condescending.

'Of course.'

'I assume, then, that it's from one of the smaller vineyards?'

'Maybe it is, Richard. And then again, maybe it isn't.'

'But it's a good year? One of the great years?'

'Yes, I guarantee that.'

'Then it shouldn't be too difficult,' Richard Pratt said, drawling
his words, looking exceedingly bored. Except that, to me, there
was something strange about his drawling and his boredom:
between the eyes a shadow of something evil, and in his bearing an
intentness that gave me a faint sense of uneasiness as I watched him.

'This one is really rather difficult,' Mike said. 'I won't force you
to bet on this one.'

'Indeed. And why not?' Again the slow arching of the brows,
the cool, intent look.

'Because it's difficult.'

'That's not very complimentary to me, you know.'

'My dear man,' Mike said, 'I'll bet you with pleasure, if that's
what you wish.'

'It shouldn't be too hard to name it.'

'You mean you want to bet?'

'I'm perfectly willing to bet,' Richard Pratt said.

'All right then, we'll have the usual. A case of the wine itself.'

'You don't think I'll be able to name it, do you.'

'As a matter of fact, and with all due respect, I don't,' Mike
said. He was making some effort to remain polite, but Pratt was

not bothering overmuch to conceal his contempt for the whole proceeding. And yet, curiously, his next question seemed to betray a certain interest.

'You like to increase the bet?'

'No, Richard. A case is plenty.'

'Would you like to bet fifty cases?'

'That would be silly.'

Mike stood very still behind his chair at the head of the table, carefully holding the bottle in its ridiculous wicker basket. There was a trace of whiteness around his nostrils now, and his mouth was shut very tight.

Pratt was lolling back in his chair, looking up at him, the eyebrows raised, the eyes half closed, a little smile touching the corners of his lips. And again I saw, or thought I saw, something distinctly disturbing about the man's face, that shadow of intentness between the eyes, and in the eyes themselves, right in their centres where it was black, a small slow spark of shrewdness, hiding.

'So you don't want to increase the bet?'

'As far as I'm concerned, old man, I don't give a damn,' Mike said. 'I'll bet you anything you like.'

The three women and I sat quietly, watching the two men. Mike's wife was becoming annoyed; her mouth had gone sour and I felt that at any moment she was going to interrupt. Our roast beef lay before us on our plates, slowly steaming.

'So you'll bet me anything I like?'

'That's what I told you. I'll bet you anything you damn well please, if you want to make an issue out of it.'

'Even ten thousand pounds?'

'Certainly I will, if that's the way you want it.' Mike was more confident now. He knew quite well that he could call any sum Pratt cared to mention.

'So you say I can name the bet?' Pratt asked again.

'That's what I said.'

There was a pause while Pratt looked slowly around the table, first at me, then at the three women, each in turn. He appeared to be reminding us that we were witness to the offer.

'Mike!' Mrs Schofield said. 'Mike, why don't we stop this nonsense and eat our food. It's getting cold.'

'But it isn't nonsense,' Pratt told her evenly. 'We're making a little bet.'

I noticed the maid standing in the background holding a dish of vegetables, wondering whether to come forward with them or not.

'All right, then,' Pratt said. 'I'll tell you what I want you to bet.'

'Come on, then,' Mike said, rather reckless. 'I don't give a damn what it is – you're on.'

Pratt nodded, and again the little smile moved the corners of his lips, and then, quite slowly, looking at Mike all the time, he said, 'I want you to bet me the hand of your daughter in marriage.'

Louise Schofield gave a jump. 'Hey!' she cried. 'No! That's not funny! Look here, Daddy, that's not funny at all.'

'No, dear,' her mother said. 'They're only joking.'

'I'm not joking,' Richard Pratt said.

'It's ridiculous,' Mike said. He was off balance again now.

'You said you'd bet anything I liked.'

'I meant money.'

'You didn't *say* money.'

'That's what I meant.'

'Then it's a pity you didn't say it. But anyway, if you wish to go back on your offer, that's quite all right with me.'

'It's not a question of going back on my offer, old man. It's a no-bet anyway, because you can't match the stake. You yourself don't happen to have a daughter to put up against mine in case you lose. And if you had, I wouldn't want to marry her.'

'I'm glad of that, dear,' his wife said.

'I'll put up anything you like,' Pratt announced. 'My house, for example. How about my house?'

'Which one?' Mike asked, joking now.

'The country one.'

'Why not the other one as well?'

'All right then, if you wish it. Both my houses.'

At that point I saw Mike pause. He took a step forward and placed the bottle in its basket gently down on the table. He moved the salt-cellar to one side, then the pepper, and then he picked up his knife, studied the blade thoughtfully for a moment, and put it down again. His daughter, too, had seen him pause.

'Now, Daddy!' she cried. 'Don't be *absurd*! It's *too* silly for words. I refuse to be betted on like this.'

'Quite right, dear,' her mother said. 'Stop it at once, Mike, and sit down and eat your food.'

Mike ignored her. He looked over at his daughter and he smiled, a slow, fatherly, protective smile. But in his eyes, suddenly, there glimmered a little triumph. 'You know,' he said, smiling as he spoke. 'You know, Louise, we ought to think about this a bit.'

'Now, stop it, Daddy! I refuse even to listen to you! Why, I've never heard anything so ridiculous in my life!'

'No, seriously, my dear. Just wait a moment and hear what I have to say.'

'But I don't *want* to hear it.'

'Louise! Please! It's like this. Richard, here, has offered us a serious bet. He is the one who wants to make it, not me. And if he loses, he will have to hand over a considerable amount of property. Now, wait a minute, my dear, don't interrupt. The point is this. *He cannot possibly win.*'

'He seems to think he can.'

'Now listen to me, because I know what I'm talking about. The expert, when tasting a claret – so long as it is not one of the famous great wines like Lafite or Latour – can only get a certain way towards naming the vineyard. He can, of course, tell you the Bordeaux district from which the wine comes, whether it is from St Emilion, Pomerol, Graves, or Médoc. But then each district had several communes, little counties, and each county has many, many small vineyards. It is impossible for a man to differentiate between them all by taste and smell alone. I don't mind telling you that this one I've got here is a wine from a small vineyard that is surrounded by many other small vineyards, and he'll never get it. It's impossible.'

'You can't be sure of that,' his daughter said.

'I'm telling you I can. Though I say it myself, I understand quite a bit about this wine business, you know. And anyway, heavens alive, girl, I'm your father and you don't think I'd let you in for – for something you didn't want, do you? I'm trying to make you some money.'

'Mike!' his wife said sharply. 'Stop it now, Mike, please!'

Again he ignored her. 'If you will take this bet,' he said to his daughter, 'in ten minutes you will be the owner of two large houses.'

'But I don't want two large houses, Daddy.'

'Then sell them. Sell them back to him on the spot. I'll arrange all that for you. And then, just think of it, my dear, you'll be rich! You'll be independent for the rest of your life!'

'Oh, Daddy, I don't like it. I think it's silly.'

'So do I,' the mother said. She jerked her head briskly up and down as she spoke, like a hen. 'You ought to be ashamed of yourself, Michael, ever suggesting such a thing! Your own daughter, too!'

Mike didn't even look at her. 'Take it!' he said eagerly, staring hard at the girl. 'Take it, quick! I'll guarantee you won't lose.'

'But I don't like it, Daddy.'

'Come on, girl. Take it!'

Mike was pushing her hard. He was leaning towards her, fixing her with two hard bright eyes, and it was not easy for the daughter to resist him.

'But what if I lose?'

'I keep telling you, you can't lose. I'll guarantee it.'

'Oh, Daddy, must I?'

'I'm making you a fortune. So come on now. What do you say, Louise? All right?'

For the last time, she hesitated. Then she gave a helpless little shrug of the shoulders and said, 'Oh, all right, then. Just so long as you swear there's no danger of losing.'

'Good!' Mike cried. 'That's fine! Then it's a bet!'

'Yes,' Richard Pratt said, looking at the girl. 'It's a bet.'

Immediately, Mike picked up the wine, tipped the first thimbleful* into his own glass, then skipped excitedly around the table filling up the others. Now everyone was watching Richard Pratt, watching his face as he reached slowly for his glass with his right hand and lifted it to his nose. The man was about fifty years old and he did not have a pleasant face. Somehow, it was all mouth – mouth and lips – the full, wet lips of the professional gourmet, the lower lip hanging downward in the centre, a pendulous, permanently open taster's lip, shaped open to receive the rim of a glass or a morsel of food. Like a keyhole, I thought, watching it; his mouth is like a large wet keyhole.

Slowly he lifted the glass to his nose. The point of the nose entered the glass and moved over the surface of the wine, delicately sniffing. He swirled the wine gently around in the glass to receive the bouquet. His concentration was intense. He had closed his eyes, and now the whole top half of his body, the head and neck and chest, seemed to become a kind of huge sensitive smelling-machine, receiving, filtering, analysing the message from the sniffing nose.

Mike, I noticed, was lounging in his chair, apparently unconcerned, but he was watching every move. Mrs Schofield, the wife, sat prim and upright at the other end of the table, looking straight ahead, her face tight with disapproval. The daughter, Louise, had shifted her chair away a little, and sidewise*, facing the gourmet, and she, like her father, was watching closely.

For at least a minute, the smelling process continued; then, without opening his eyes or moving his head, Pratt lowered the glass to his mouth and tipped in almost half the contents. He paused, his mouth full of wine, getting the first taste; then, he permitted some of it to trickle down his throat and I saw his Adam's apple move as it passed by. But most of it he retained in his mouth. And now, without swallowing again, he drew in through his lips a thin breath of air which mingled with the fumes of the wine in the mouth and passed on down into his lungs. He held the breath, blew it out through his nose, and finally began to roll the wine around under the tongue, and chewed it, actually chewed it with his teeth as though it were bread.

It was a solemn, impassive performance, and I must say he did it well.

'Um,' he said, putting down the glass, running a pink tongue over his lips. 'Um – yes. A very interesting little wine – gentle and gracious, almost feminine in the after-taste.'

There was an excess of saliva in his mouth, and as he spoke he spat an occasional bright speck of it on to the table.

'Now we can start to eliminate,' he said. 'You will pardon me for doing this carefully, but there is much at stake. Normally I would perhaps take a bit of a chance, leaping forward quickly and landing right in the middle of the vineyard of my choice. But this time – I must move cautiously this time, must I not?' He looked up at Mike and smiled, a thick-lipped, wet-lipped smile. Mike did not smile back.

'First, then, which district in Bordeaux does this wine come from? That's not too difficult to guess. It is far too light in the body to be from either St Emilion or Graves. It is obviously a Médoc. There's no doubt about *that*.

'Now – from which commune in Médoc does it come? That also, by elimination, should not be too difficult to decide. Margaux? No. It cannot be Margaux. It has not the violent bouquet of a Margaux. Pauillac? It cannot be Pauillac, either. It is too tender, too gentle and wistful for Pauillac. The wine of Pauillac has a character that is almost imperious in its taste. And also, to me, a Pauillac contains just a little pith, a curious dusty, pithy flavour that the grape acquires from the soil of the district. No, no. This – this is a very gentle wine, demure and bashful in the first taste, emerging shyly but quite graciously in the second. A little arch, perhaps, in the second taste, and a little naughty also, teasing the tongue with a trace, just a trace of tannin. Then, in the after-taste, delightful – consoling and feminine, with a certain blithely generous quality that one associates only with the wines of the commune of St Julien. Unmistakably this is a St Julien.'

He leaned back in his chair, held his hands up level with his chest, and placed the fingertips carefully together. He was becoming ridiculously pompous, but I thought that some of it was deliberate, simply to mock his host. I found myself waiting rather tensely for him to go on. The girl Louise was lighting a cigarette. Pratt heard the match strike and he turned to her, flaring suddenly with real anger. 'Please!' he said. 'Please don't do that! It's a disgusting habit, to smoke at table!'

She looked up at him, still holding the burning match in one hand, the big slow eyes settling on his face, resting there a moment, moving away again, slow and contemptuous. She bent her head and blew out the match, but continued to hold the unlighted cigarette in her fingers.

'I'm sorry, my dear,' Pratt said, 'but I simply cannot have smoking at table.'

She didn't look at him again.

'Now, let me see – where were we?' he said. 'Ah, yes. This wine is from Bordeaux, from the commune of St Julien, in the district of Médoc. So far, so good. But now we come to the more difficult part – the name of the vineyard itself. For in St Julien there are many vineyards, and as our host so rightly remarked earlier on, there is often not much difference between the wine of one and the wine of another. But we shall see.'

He paused again, closing his eyes. ' I am trying to establish the "growth",' he said. 'If I can do that, it will be half the battle. Now, let me see. This wine is obviously not from a first-growth vineyard* – nor even a second. It is not a great wine. The quality, the – the – what do you call it? – the radiance, the power, is lacking. But a third growth – that it could be. And yet I doubt it. We know it is a good year – our host has said so – and this is probably flattering it a little bit. I must be careful. I must be very careful here.'

He picked up his glass and took another small sip.

'Yes,' he said, sucking his lips, 'I was right. It is a fourth growth. Now I am sure of it. A fourth growth from a very good year – from a great year, in fact. And that's what made it taste for a moment like a third – or even a second-growth wine. Good! That's better! Now we are closing in! What are the fourth-growth vineyards in the commune of St Julien?'

Again he paused, took up his glass, and held the rim against that sagging, pendulous lower lip of his. Then I saw the tongue shoot out, pink and narrow, the tip of it dipping into the wine, withdrawing swiftly again – a repulsive sight. When he lowered the glass, his eyes remained closed, the face concentrated, only the lips moving, sliding over each other like two pieces of wet, spongy rubber.

'There it is again!' he cried. 'Tannin in the middle taste, and the quick astringent squeeze upon the tongue. Yes, yes, of course! Now I have it! The wine comes from one of those small vineyards around Beychevelle. I remember now. The Beychevelle district, and the river and the little harbour that has silted up so the wine ships can no longer use it. Beychevelle . . . could it actually be a Beychevelle itself? No, I don't think so. Not quite. But it is somewhere very close. Château Talbot? Could it be Talbot? Yes, it could. Wait one moment.'

He sipped the wine again, and out of the side of my eye I noticed Mike Schofield and how he was leaning farther and farther forward over the table, his mouth slightly open, his small eyes fixed upon Richard Pratt.

'No. I was wrong. It is not a Talbot. A Talbot comes forward to you just a little quicker than this one, the fruit is nearer the surface. If it is a '34, which I believe it is, then it couldn't be Talbot. Well, well. Let me think. It is not a Beychevelle and it is not a Talbot, and yet – yet it is so close to both of them, so close, that the vineyard must be almost in between. Now, which could that be?'

He hesitated, and we waited, watching his face. Everyone, even Mike's wife, was watching him now. I heard the maid put down the dish of vegetables on the sideboard behind me, gently, so as not to disturb the silence.

'Ah!' he cried. 'I have it! Yes, I think I have it!'

For the last time, he sipped the wine. Then, still holding the glass up near his mouth, he turned to Mike and he smiled, a slow, silky smile, and he said, 'You know what this is? This is the little Château Branaire-Ducru.'

Mike sat tight, not moving.

'And the year, 1934.'

We all looked at Mike, waiting for him to turn the bottle around in its basket and show the label.

'Is that your final answer?' Mike said.

'Yes, I think so.'

'Well, is it or isn't it?'

'Yes, it is.'

'What was the name again?'

'Château Branaire-Ducru. Pretty little vineyard. Lovely old château. Know it quite well. Can't think why I didn't recognize it at once.'

'Come on, Daddy,' the girl said. 'Turn it round and let's have a peek. I want my two houses.'

'Just a minute,' Mike said. 'Wait just a minute.' He was sitting very quiet, bewildered-looking, and his face was becoming puffy and pale, as though all the force was draining slowly out of him.

'Michael!' his wife called sharply from the other end of the table. 'What's the matter?'

'Keep out of this, Margaret, will you please.'

Richard Pratt was looking at Mike, smiling with his mouth, his eyes small and bright. Mike was not looking at anyone.

'Daddy!' the daughter cried, agonized. 'But, Daddy, you don't mean to say he's guessed it right!'

'Now, stop worrying, my dear,' Mike said. 'There's nothing to worry about.'

I think it was more to get away from his family than anything else that Mike then turned to Richard Pratt and said, 'I'll tell you what, Richard. I think you and I better slip off into the next room and have a little chat.'

'I don't want a little chat,' Pratt said. 'All I want is to see the label on that bottle.' He knew he was a winner now; he had the bearing, the quiet arrogance of a winner, and I could see that he was prepared to become thoroughly nasty if there was any trouble. 'What are you waiting for?' he said to Mike. 'Go on and turn it round.'

Then this happened: the maid, the tiny, erect figure of the maid in her white-and-black uniform, was standing beside Richard Pratt, holding something out in her hand. 'I believe these are yours, sir,' she said.

Pratt glanced around, saw the pair of thin horn-rimmed spectacles that she held out to him, and for a moment he hesitated. 'Are they? Perhaps they are, I don't know.'

'Yes, sir, they're yours.' The maid was an elderly woman – nearer seventy than sixty – a faithful family retainer of many years' standing. She put the spectacles down on the table beside him.

Without thanking her, Pratt took them up and slipped them into his top pocket, behind the white handkerchief.

But the maid didn't go away. She remained standing beside and slightly behind Richard Pratt, and there was something so unusual in her manner and in the way she stood there, small, motionless and erect, that I for one found myself watching her with a sudden apprehension. Her old grey face had a frosty, determined look, the lips were compressed, the little chin was out, and the hands were clasped together tight before her. The curious cap on her head and the flash of white down the front of her uniform made her seem like some tiny, ruffled, white-breasted bird.

'You left them in Mr Schofield's study,' she said. Her voice was unnaturally, deliberately polite. 'On top of the green filing cabinet in his study, sir, when you happened to go in there by yourself before dinner.'

It took a few moments for the full meaning of her words to penetrate, and in the silence that followed I became aware of Mike and how he was slowly drawing himself up in his chair, and the colour coming to his face, and the eyes opening wide, and the curl of the mouth, and the dangerous little patch of whiteness beginning to spread around the area of the nostrils.

'Now, Michael!' his wife said. 'Keep calm now, Michael, dear! Keep calm!'

Notes

jobber   (p23)
> someone who buys and sells stocks on behalf of someone else

thimbleful   (p31)
> a very small amount

sidewise   (p32)
> sideways

first growth vineyard   (p34)
> a vineyard of the highest quality, followed in rank by second growth, third growth, etc.

Discussion

1 How do you think Pratt's attitude to wine differs from his attitude to people? What does this reveal about his character?

2 Why does the maid wait as long as she does to come forward with the spectacles? What is her attitude towards Pratt, and how does the author reveal it to the reader?

3 What should the result of the bet be? Should Louise be entitled to Pratt's houses? Is the bet cancelled by Pratt's cheating? Give your opinion and explain your reasoning.

4 How do women feature in this story? What attitudes do they have, and what actions do they take, compared with those of the men?

5 What human characteristics (greed, deception, pride, etc.) do you associate with the different characters in the story? Do you think the characters are convincing? Which of them do you find sympathetic?

Language Focus

1 Throughout the story attention is repeatedly drawn to Pratt's lips. Study the following descriptions in context. Why do you think the author chose this part of the body in particular, and what effect does this repetition have? How do these descriptions contribute to your view of Pratt?

- *the wet lower lip, suddenly imperious and ugly* (p26)
- *the full, wet lips of the professional gourmet*   (p31)
- *his mouth is like a large, wet keyhole* (p31)

- *running a pink tongue over his lips* (p32)
- *a thick-lipped, wet-lipped smile* (p33)
- *that sagging, pendulous lower lip of his* (p34)
- *the lips moving, sliding over each other like two pieces of wet, spongy rubber* (p35)
- *a slow, silky smile* (p35)

Now look back at the story and find references to Pratt's eyes. What do these add to the picture you have formed of him?

2 *His round jovial face seemed to loosen slightly and to sag, but he contained himself and was still and said nothing.* (p24/25)
What does this reveal about Mike's reaction to Pratt's behaviour? How does this incident pave the way for what happens with the second bottle of wine?

3 *. . . he reached for his glass, and in two short swallows he tipped the wine down his throat and turned immediately to resume his conversation with Louise Schofield.* (p24)
Pratt is a gourmet who appreciates wine. So what is the significance of the way he drinks his wine here?

ACTIVITIES

1 The story ends with feelings at a high pitch. What do you think will happen next? Will the two men fight? Will Pratt try to buy Mike's silence, fearing for his reputation? What about the bet? Write a paragraph explaining the conclusion of these events as you see them.

2 Imagine that the guests have left and Mike and his wife are now alone. What do they say to each other? What explanation can Mike offer for his behaviour, and how does his wife respond to this? Write the conversation between them.

3 Suppose a newspaper finds out about these events and reports on them. Write the letters that both men send defending themselves – Mike complaining of the abuse of his home and hospitality, and Pratt laughing it off as a joke between friends.

4 Change the story so that it is either the narrator's wife, or Mike's wife, or Louise who produces the spectacles. How would this throw a different light on the behaviour of these women up to this point?

TELLING STORIES

THE AUTHOR

Maeve Binchy was born in Dublin in 1940. After school and university in Ireland she became a teacher, and then joined the *Irish Times* as a journalist in 1969. She is now based in London. She has written plays for the stage and for television, and is the author of many bestsellers, both novels and volumes of short stories. Among her novels are *Light a Penny Candle, Firefly Summer, The Copper Beech*, and *Tara Road*. Her novel *Circle of Friends* was made into a film in 1995. Her short-story collections include *Central Line, Victoria Line, The Lilac Bus*, and *Dublin 4*. Maeve Binchy's stories give an affectionate and carefully observed picture of ordinary people, often at crucial moments of their lives.

THE STORY

Before you take a major step in your life – starting a new job, getting married, moving to another country – it's only natural to have doubts. Is this the right thing to do? The right time? The right place? The right person? Is this a real doubt, or just a moment's nervousness? Eventually you decide, and life goes on – forever different because of the decision you have made.

On the evening before the day when Andrew and Irene are due to be married, he arrives at her house with terrible news. Irene listens to him, calm and thoughtful, but says nothing. When she finally speaks, she must be very careful to say the right thing . . .

TELLING STORIES

People always said that Irene had total recall. She seemed to remember the smallest details of things they had long forgotten – the words of old pop songs, the shades of old lipsticks, minute-by-minute reconstructions of important events like Graduation Day, or people's weddings. If ever you wanted a step-by-step account of times past, they said to each other: ask Irene.

Irene rarely took herself through the evening before the day she was due to be married. But if she had to then she could have done it with no difficulty. It wasn't hard to remember the smells: the lilac in the garden, the polish on all the furniture, the orange blossom in the house. She even remembered the rich smell of the hand-cream that she was massaging carefully into her hands when she heard the doorbell ring. It must be a late present, she thought, or possibly yet another fussy aunt who had come up from the country for the ceremony and arrived like a homing pigeon at the house.

She was surprised to hear Andrew's voice, talking to her younger sister downstairs. Andrew was meant to be at his home dealing with all his relations just as Irene had been doing. He had an uncle, a priest, flying in from the African Missions to assist at the wedding. Andrew's grandmother was a demanding old lady who regarded every gathering as in some way centring around her; Irene was surprised that Andrew had been allowed to escape.

Rosemary, her sister and one of the bridesmaids, had no interest in anything apart from the possible appearance of a huge spot on her face. She waved Andrew airily up the stairs.

'She's been up there titivating herself for hours,' Irene heard her say. Before she had time to react to Rosemary's tactlessness, Irene heard Andrew say 'Oh God,' in a funny, choked sort of voice, and before he even came into the room, she knew something was very wrong.

Andrew's face was as white as the dress that hung between sheets of tissue paper on the outside of the big mahogany wardrobe. His hands shook and trembled like the branches of the beautiful laburnum tree outside her window, the yellow blossom shaking in the summer breeze.

He tried to take her hand but she was covered in hand-cream. Irene decided that somehow it was imperative that she keep rubbing the cream still further in. It was like not walking on the crack in the road*: if she kept massaging her hands then he couldn't take them in his, and he couldn't tell her what awful thing he was about to tell her.

On and on she went rhythmically, almost hypnotically, as if she were pulling on tight gloves. Her hands never stopped moving; her face never moved at all.

He fumbled for words, but Irene didn't help him.

The words came eventually, tumbling over each other, contradicting each other even, punctuated with apology and self-disgust. It wasn't that there was anyone else, Lord no, and it wasn't even as if he had stopped loving her, in many ways he had never loved her more than now, looking at her and knowing that he was destroying all their dreams and their hopes, but he had thought about it very seriously, and the truth was that he wasn't ready, he wasn't old enough, maybe technically he was old enough, but in his heart he didn't feel old enough to settle down, he wasn't certain enough that this was the Right Thing. For either of them, he added hastily, wanting Irene to know that it was in her interests as well as his.

On and on, she worked the cream into her hands and wrists; even a little way up her arms.

She sat impassively on her little blue bedroom-stool, her frilly dressing-table behind her. There were no tears, no tantrums. There were not even any words. Eventually he could speak no more.

'Oh Irene, say something for God's sake, tell me how much you hate me, what I've done to your life.' He almost begged to be railed against.

She spoke slowly, her voice was very calm. 'But of course I don't hate you,' she said, as if explaining something to a slow-witted child. 'I love you, I always will, and let's look at what you've done to my life . . . You've changed it certainly . . .' Her eyes fell on the wedding dress.

Andrew started again. Guilt and shame poured from him in a torrent released by her unexpected gentleness. He would take it upon himself to explain to everyone, he would tell her parents now. He would explain everything to the guests, he would see that the presents were returned. He would try to compensate her family financially for all the expense they had gone to. If everyone thought this was the right thing to do he would go abroad, to a faraway place like Australia or Canada or Africa . . . somewhere they needed young lawyers, a place where nobody from here need ever look at him again and remember all the trouble he had caused.

And then suddenly he realised that he and he alone was doing the talking; Irene sat still, apart from those curious hand movements, as if she had not heard or understood what he was saying. A look of horror came over his face: perhaps she did not understand.

'I mean it, Irene,' he said simply. 'I really do mean it, you know, I wish I didn't.'

'I know you mean it.' Her voice was steady, her eyes were clear. She did understand.

Andrew clutched at a straw. 'Perhaps *you* feel the same. Perhaps we *both* want to get out of it? Is that what you are saying?' He was so eager to believe it, his face almost shone with enthusiasm.

But there was no quarter here. In a voice that didn't shake, with no hint of a tear in her eye, Irene said that she loved him and would always love him. But that it was far better, if he felt he couldn't go through with it, that this should be discovered the night before the marriage, rather than the night after. This way at least one of them would be free to make a different marriage when the time came.

'Well both of us, surely?' Andrew was bewildered.

Irene shook her head. 'I can't see myself marrying anyone else but you,' she said. There was no blame, regret, accusation. Just a statement.

In the big house, where three hundred guests were expected tomorrow, it was curiously silent. Perhaps the breeze had died down; they couldn't even hear the flapping of the edges of the marquee on the lawn.

The silence was too long between them. But Andrew knew she was not going to break it. 'So what will we do? First, I mean?' he asked her.

She looked at him pleasantly as if he had asked what record he should put on the player. She said nothing.

'Tell our parents, I suppose, yours first. Are they downstairs?' he suggested.

'No, they're over at the golf club, they're having a little reception or drink or something for those who aren't coming tomorrow.'

'Oh God,' Andrew said.

There was another silence.

'Do you think we should go and tell *my* parents then? Grandmother will need some time to get adjusted . . .'

Irene considered this. 'Possibly,' she said. But it was unsatisfactory.

'Or maybe the caterers,' Andrew said. 'I saw them bustling around setting things up . . .' His voice broke. He seemed about to cry. 'Oh God, Irene, it's a terrible mess.'

'I know,' she agreed, as if they were talking about a rain-cloud or some other unavoidable irritation to the day.

'And I suppose I should tell Martin, he's been fussing so much about the etiquette of it all and getting things in the right order. In a way he may be relieved . . .' Andrew gave a nervous little laugh but hastily corrected himself. 'But sorry, of course, mainly sorry, of course, very, very sorry that things haven't worked out.'

'Yes. Of course,' Irene agreed politely.

'And the bridesmaids? Don't you think we should tell Rosemary now, and Catherine? And that you should ring Rita and tell her . . . and tell her . . . that . . . well that . . .'

'Tell her what, exactly?'

'Well, tell her that we've changed our minds . . .'

'That you've changed your mind, to be strictly honest,' Irene said.

'Yes, but you agree,' he pleaded.

'What do I agree?'

'That if it is the Wrong Thing to do, then it were better we know now than tomorrow when it's all too late and we are man and wife till death . . .' his voice ran out.

'Ah yes, but don't you see, I don't think we *are* doing the Wrong Thing getting married.'

'But you agreed . . .' He was in a panic.

'Oh, of course I agreed, Andrew, I mean what on earth would be the point of not agreeing? Naturally we can't go through with it. But that's not to say that *I'm* calling it off.'

'No, no, but does that matter as much as telling people . . . I mean now that we know that it won't take place, isn't it unfair to people to let them think that it will?'

'Yes and no.'

'But we can't have them making the food, getting dressed . . .'

'I know.' She was thoughtful.

'I want to do what's best, what's the most fair,' Andrew said. And he did, Irene could see that, in the situation which he had brought about, he still wanted to be fair.

'Let's see,' she suggested. 'Who is going to be most hurt by all this?'

He thought about it. 'Your parents probably, they've gone to all this trouble . . .' He waved towards the garden where three hundred merrymakers had planned to stroll.

'No, I don't think they're the most hurt.'

'Well, maybe my uncle, the whole way back from Africa and he had to ask permission from a bishop. Or my grandmother . . . or the bridesmaids. They won't get a chance to dress up.' Andrew struggled to be fair.

'I think that I am the one who will be most hurt.' Irene's voice wasn't even slightly raised. It was as if she had given the problem equally dispassionate judgement.

'I mean, my parents have other daughters. There'll be Rosemary and Catherine, one day they'll have weddings. And your uncle, the priest . . . well he'll have a bit of a holiday. No, I think I am the one who is *most* upset, I'm not going to marry the man I love, have the life I thought I was going to.'

'I know, I know.' He sounded like someone sympathising over a bereavement.

'So I thought that perhaps you'd let me handle it *my* way.'

'Of course, Irene, that's why I'm here, whatever you say.'

'I say we shouldn't tell anyone anything. Not tonight.'

'I won't change my mind, in case that's what you're thinking.'

'Lord no, why should you? It's much too serious to be flitting about, chopping and changing.'

He handed their future into her hands. 'Do it whatever way you
want. Just let me know and I'll do it.' He was prepared to pay any
price to get the wedding called off.

But Irene didn't allow herself the time to think about that. 'Let
me be the one not to turn up,' she said. 'Let me be seen to be the
partner who had second thoughts. That way at least I get out of it
with some dignity.'

He agreed. Grooms had been left standing at the altar* before.
He would always say afterwards that he had been greatly hurt but
he respected Irene's decision.

'And you won't tell *anyone?*' she made him promise.

'Maybe Martin?' he suggested.

'Particularly not Martin, he'd give the game away. In the church
you must be seen to be waiting for me.'

'But your father and mother . . . is it fair to leave it to the last
minute?'

'They'd prefer to think that I let you down rather than the other
way. Who wants a daughter who has been abandoned by the
groom?'

'It's not that . . .' he began.

'I *know* that, silly, but not everyone else does.' She had stopped
creaming her hands. They talked like old friends and conspirators.
The thing would only succeed if nobody had an inkling.

'And afterwards . . .' He seemed very eager to know every step
of her plan.

'Afterwards . . .' Irene was thoughtful. 'Oh, afterwards we can
go along being friends . . . until you meet someone else . . . People
will admire you, think you are very forgiving, too tolerant even . . .
there'll be no awkwardness. No embarrassment.'

Andrew stood at the gate of the big house to wave goodbye; she
sat by her window under the great laburnum tree and waved back.
She was a girl in a million. What a pity he hadn't met her later. Or

proposed to her later, when he was *ready* to be married. His stomach lurched at the thought of the mayhem they were about to unleash the following day. He went home with a heavy heart to hear stories of the Missions from his uncle the priest, and tales of long-gone grandeur from his grandmother.

∽

Martin had read many books on being Best Man. Possibly too many.

'It's only natural for you to be nervous,' he said to Andrew at least forty times. 'It's only natural for you to worry about your speech, but remember the most important thing is to thank Irene's parents for giving her to you.'

When they heard the loud sniffs from Andrew's grandmother, the Best Man had soothing remarks also. 'It's only natural for elderly females to cry at weddings,' he said.

Andrew stood there, his stomach like lead. Since marriage was instituted, no groom had stood like this in the certain knowledge that his bride was not just a little late, or held up in traffic, or adjusting her veil – all the excuses that Martin was busy hissing into his ear.

He felt a shame like he had never known, allowing all these three hundred people to assemble in a church for a ceremony that would not take place. He looked fearfully at the parish priest, and at his own uncle. It took some seconds for it to sink in that the congregation had risen to its feet, and that the organist had crashed into the familiar chords of 'Here Comes The Bride*'.

He turned like any groom turns and saw Irene, perfectly at ease on her father's arm, smiling to the left and smiling to the right.

With his mouth wide open and his face whiter than the dress she wore, he looked into her eyes. He felt Martin's fingers in his ribs and he stepped forward to stand beside her.

∽

Despite her famous recall, Irene never told that story to anyone. She only talked about it once to Andrew, on their honeymoon, when he tried to go over the events himself. And in all the years that followed, it had been so obvious that she had taken the right decision, run the right risk and realised that their marriage was the Right Thing, there was no point in talking about it at all.

NOTES

not walking on the crack in the road   (p43)
>   superstitious people believe that not stepping on cracks and holes in
>   the road saves them from various unpleasant fates

left standing at the altar   (p48)
>   left waiting in church for a bride or bridegroom who has changed
>   their mind about getting married

Here Comes the Bride   (p49)
>   traditional song played when the bride enters the church where she is
>   to be married

DISCUSSION

1   At what point in the story does Irene stop creaming her hands? What is
    the significance of this?

2   Silence occurs at a number of points in the story. Why do you think it
    comes about, and what do you think is going on meanwhile in the
    minds of the characters?

3   Which character do you feel most sympathy for? Irene shows little
    emotion in response to Andrew's shocking news; do you find her cold
    and calculating, or is she simply trying to hold onto the man she loves
    by using her wits? Is Andrew just nervous and tactless, or a shallow
    idiot?

4   Was it, in the end, the Right Thing to do? Was Andrew just suffering
    from nerves? Was Irene right to take the chance that she did? Does the
    fact that they are still married, years later, prove she was right?

5   Can any relationship survive when based on a deception like this?
    Does a close relationship like marriage demand complete honesty
    between the partners, or do people accept small lies and deceptions as
    necessities, or at least an unavoidable part of human life?

LANGUAGE FOCUS

1   Rephrase these expressions from the story in your own words.

>   *Irene had total recall*   (p42)
>   *Andrew clutched at a straw*   (p44)
>   *'That's not to say that* I'm *calling it off'*   (p46)

> *He was prepared to pay any price* (p48)
> *She was a girl in a million* (p48)
> *He went home with a heavy heart* (p49)
> *his stomach like lead* (p49)

2 How do the following extracts take on an additional meaning on second reading, after you know how the story ends?

- *'. . . now that we know it won't take place, isn't it unfair to people to let them think that it will?'*
  'Yes and no.' (p46/47)
- *He handed their future into her hands.* (p48)
- *He was prepared to pay any price to get the wedding called off. But Irene didn't allow herself the time to think about that.* (p48)
- *They talked like old friends and conspirators. The thing would only succeed if nobody had an inkling.* (p48)

ACTIVITIES

1 Write the conversation that takes place between Andrew and Irene 'on their honeymoon, when he tried to go over the events himself.' How do you think Irene explained herself? Would she lie to Andrew about what they had agreed at their meeting? Would she tell him that she had always intended to be at the church, because she knew it was the 'right thing'? Or would she pretend that she had intended not to go, and only decided at the last minute? What would be the best way of persuading Andrew to accept what had happened?

2 *'Irene never told that story to anyone.'* If she did decide to tell the story to a close friend, what would she say? How do you think she might describe what was going on in her mind at different moments?

3 At the end of the story it seems that Andrew accepts that Irene did the right thing. But suppose he finds that he was right after all and that the marriage was a mistake? Suggest how the end of the story might be rewritten in this case.

4 Irene tells Andrew not to tell Martin. Suppose that he does tell Martin after all. What do you think Martin might say?

5 The title *Telling Stories* works on two levels. What are they? Do you think it is an effective title? What other title could you suggest?

The Coward

The Author

V. S. Naipaul was born in Trinidad in 1932. He studied at Oxford and worked in Britain as a journalist before publishing his first novel, *The Mystic Masseur*, in 1957. He made his name in 1961 with the satirical novel *A House for Mr Biswas*, which is set in Trinidad. In later books humour gave way to an honest and often highly critical view of the places that he lived in or visited. He has written a large number of successful novels; these include *In a Free State,* which won the Booker Prize in 1971, and *The Enigma of Arrival,* which draws on his own experience of leaving Trinidad and coming to England. He has also written short stories, travel books and other non-fiction works. Naipaul was knighted in 1990, and won the Nobel Prize for Literature in 2001.

The Story

'Cowardly dogs bark loudest,' wrote the playwright John Webster four hundred years ago, and there are still plenty of noisy bullies around today – bullies who are too cowardly to carry out their threats when challenged. But you don't have to make a lot of noise to create a fearsome reputation for yourself. If you are big, and you look tough and dangerous, people's imaginations will create it for you. Before you know it, everyone is afraid of you – whether they have reason to be or not.

The scene is Trinidad in World War II, and the boys of Miguel Street are both proud of Big Foot and terrified of him. People look at Big Foot – huge, grim, and dangerous-looking – and decide they just don't want to fight. But Big Foot has a secret . . .

THE COWARD

Big Foot was really big and really black, and everybody in Miguel Street was afraid of him. It wasn't his bigness or his blackness that people feared, for there were blacker and bigger people about. People were afraid of him because he was so silent and sulky; he *looked* dangerous, like those terrible dogs that never bark but just look at you from the corner of their eyes.

Hat used to say, 'Is only a form of showing off, you know, all this quietness he does give us. He quiet just because he ain't have anything to say, that's all.'

Yet you could hear Hat telling all sorts of people at the races and cricket, 'Big Foot and me? We is bosom pals, man. We grow up together.'

And at school I myself used to say, 'Big Foot does live in my street, you hear. I know him good good*, and if any one of all you touch me, I go tell Big Foot.'

At that time I had never spoken a single word to Big Foot.

We in Miguel Street were proud to claim him because he was something of a character in Port of Spain, and had quite a reputation. It was Big Foot who flung the stone at Radio Trinidad building one day and broke a window. When the magistrate asked why he did it, Big Foot just said, 'To wake them up.'

A well-wisher paid the fine for him.

Then there was the time he got a job driving one of the diesel-buses. He drove the bus out of the city to Carenage, five miles away, and told the passengers to get out and bathe. He stood by to see that they did.

After that he got a job as a postman, and he had a great time misplacing people's letters. They found him at Dock site, with the bag half full of letters, soaking his big feet in the Gulf of Paria.

He said, 'Is hard work, walking all over the place, delivering people letters. You come like a postage stamp, man.'

All Trinidad thought of him as a comedian, but we who knew him thought otherwise.

It was people like Big Foot who gave the steel-bands a bad name. Big Foot was always ready to start a fight with another band, but he looked so big and dangerous that he himself was never involved in any fight, and he never went to jail for more than three months or so at a time.

Hat, especially, was afraid of Big Foot. Hat often said, 'I don't know why they don't lose Big Foot in jail, you know.'

You would have thought that when he was beating his pans* and dancing in the street at Carnival, Big Foot would at least smile and look happy. But no. It was on occasions like this that he prepared his sulkiest and grimmest face; and when you saw him beating a pan, you felt, to judge by his earnestness, that he was doing some sacred act.

One day a big crowd of us – Hat, Edward, Eddoes, Boyee, Errol and myself – went to the cinema. We were sitting in a row, laughing and talking all during the film, having a good time.

A voice from behind said, very quietly, 'Shut up.'

We turned and saw Big Foot.

He lazily pulled out a knife from his trouser pocket, flicked the blade open, and stuck it in the back of my chair.

He looked up at the screen and said in a frightening friendly way, 'Talk.'

We didn't say a word for the rest of the film.

Afterwards Hat said, 'You does only get policeman son behaving in that way. Policeman son and priest son.'

Boyee said, 'You mean Big Foot is priest son?'

Hat said, 'You too stupid. Priests and them does have children?'

We heard a lot about Big Foot's father from Hat. It seemed he was as much a terror as Big Foot. Sometimes when Boyee and Errol and I were comparing notes about beatings, Boyee said, 'The blows we get is nothing to what Big Foot uses to get from his father. That is how he get so big, you know. I meet a boy from Belmont the other day in the savannah, and this boy tell me that blows does make you grow.'

Errol said, 'You is a blasted fool, man. How you does let people give you stupidness like that?'

Once Hat said, 'Every day Big Foot father, the policeman, giving Big Foot blows. Like medicine. Three times a day after meals. And hear Big Foot talk afterwards. He used to say, "When I get big and have children, I go beat them, beat them." '

I didn't say it then, because I was ashamed; but I had often felt the same way when my mother beat me.

I asked Hat, 'And Big Foot mother? She used to beat him too?'

Hat said, 'Oh, God! That woulda kill him. Big Foot didn't have any mother. His father didn't married, thank God.'

The Americans were crawling all over Port of Spain in those days, making the city really hot. Children didn't take long to find out that they were easy people, always ready to give with both hands. Hat began working a small racket*. He had five of us going all over the district begging for chewing gum and chocolate. For every packet of chewing gum we gave him we got a cent. Sometimes I made as much as twelve cents in a day. Some boy told me later that Hat was selling the chewing gum for six cents a packet, but I didn't believe it.

One afternoon, standing on the pavement outside my house, I saw an American soldier down the street, coming towards me. It was about two o'clock in the afternoon, very hot, and the street was practically empty.

The American behaved in a very surprising way when I sprinted down to ask, 'Got any gum, Joe*?'

He mumbled something about begging kids and I think he was going to slap me or cuff me. He wasn't very big, but I was afraid. I think he was drunk.

He set his mouth.

A gruff voice said, 'Look, leave the boy alone, you hear.'

It was Big Foot.

Not another word was said. The American, suddenly humble, walked away, making a great pretence of not being in a hurry.

Big Foot didn't even look at me.

I never said again, 'Got any gum, Joe?'

∝

Yet this did not make me like Big Foot. I was, I believe, a little more afraid of him.

I told Hat about the American and Big Foot.

Hat said, 'All the Americans not like that. You can't throw away twelve cents a day like that.'

But I refused to beg any more.

I said, 'If it wasn't for Big Foot, the man woulda kill me.'

Hat said, 'You know, is a good thing Big Foot father dead before Big Foot really get big.'

I said, 'What happen to Big Foot father, then?'

Hat said, 'You ain't hear? It was a famous thing. A crowd of black people beat him up and kill him in 1937 when they was having the riots in the oilfields. Big Foot father was playing hero, just like Big Foot playing hero now.'

I said, 'Hat, why you don't like Big Foot?'

Hat said, 'I ain't have anything against him.'

I said, 'Why you fraid* him so, then?'

Hat said, 'Ain't you fraid him too?'

I nodded. 'But I feel you do him something and you worried.'

Hat said, 'Nothing really. It just funny. The rest of we use to give Big Foot hell too. He was thin thin when he was small, you know, and we use to have a helluva time chasing him all over the place. He couldn't run at all.'

I felt sorry for Big Foot.

I said, 'How that funny?'

Hat said, 'You go hear. You know the upshot? Big Foot come the best runner out of all of we. In the school sports he run the hundred yards in ten point four seconds. That is what they say, but you know how Trinidad people can't count time. Anyway, then we all want to come friendly* with him. But he don't want we at all at all.'

And I wondered then why Big Foot held himself back from beating Hat and the rest of the people who had bullied him when he was a boy.

But still I didn't like him.

൙

Big Foot became a carpenter for a while, and actually built two or three enormous wardrobes, rough, ugly things. But he sold them. And then he became a mason. There is no stupid pride among Trinidad craftsmen. No one is a specialist.

He came to our yard one day to do a job.

I stood by and watched him. I didn't speak to him, and he didn't speak to me. I noticed that he used his feet as a trowel. He mumbled, 'Is hard work, bending down all the time.'

He did the job well enough. His feet were not big for nothing*.

About four o'clock he knocked off, and spoke to me.

He said, 'Boy, let we go for a walk. I hot and I want to cool off.'

I didn't want to go, but I felt I had to.

We went to the sea-wall at Docksite and watched the sea. Soon it began to grow dark. The lights came on in the harbour. The world seemed very big, dark, and silent. We stood up without speaking a word.

Then a sudden sharp yap very near us tore the silence.

The suddenness and strangeness of the noise paralysed me for a moment.

It was only a dog; a small white and black dog with large flapping ears. It was dripping wet, and was wagging its tail out of pure friendliness.

I said, 'Come, boy,' and the dog shook off the water from its coat on me and then jumped all over me, yapping and squirming.

I had forgotten Big Foot, and when I looked for him I saw him about twenty yards away running for all he was worth.

I shouted, 'Is all right, Big Foot.'

But he stopped before he heard my shout.

He cried out loudly, 'Oh God, I dead, I dead. A big big bottle cut up my foot.'

I and the dog ran to him.

But when the dog came to him he seemed to forget his foot which was bleeding badly. He began hugging and stroking the wet dog, and laughing in a crazy way.

⌘

He had cut his foot very badly, and next day I saw it wrapped up. He couldn't come to finish the work he had begun in our yard.

I felt I knew more about Big Foot than any man in Miguel Street, and I was afraid that I knew so much. I felt like one of those small men in gangster films who know too much and get killed.

And thereafter I was always conscious that Big Foot knew what I was thinking. I felt his fear that I would tell.

But although I was bursting with Big Foot's secret I told no one. I would have liked to reassure him but there was no means.

His presence in the street became something that haunted me. And it was all I could do to stop myself telling Hat, 'I not fraid of Big Foot. I don't know why you fraid him so.'

⌘

Errol, Boyee, and myself sat on the pavement discussing the war.

Errol said, 'If they just make Lord Anthony Eden Prime Minister, we go beat up the Germans and them bad bad.'

Boyee said, 'What Lord Eden go do so?'

Errol just haaed, in a very knowing way.

I said, 'Yes, I always think that if they make Lord Anthony Eden Prime Minister, the war go end quick quick.'

Boyee said, 'You people just don't know the Germans. The Germans strong like hell, you know. A boy was telling me that these Germans and them could eat a nail with their teeth alone.'

Errol said, 'But we have Americans on we side now.'

Boyee said, 'But they not big like the Germans. All the Germans and them big big and strong like Big Foot, you know, and they braver than Big Foot.'

Errol said, 'Shh! Look, he coming.'

Big Foot was very near, and I felt he could hear the conversation. He was looking at me, and there was a curious look in his eyes.

Boyee said, 'Why you shhhing me so for? I ain't saying anything bad. I just saying that the Germans brave as Big Foot.'

Just for a moment, I saw the begging look in Big Foot's eyes. I looked away.

When Big Foot had passed, Errol said to me, 'Like Big Foot have something with you, boy.'

One afternoon Hat was reading the morning paper. He shouted to us, 'But look at what I reading here, man.'

We asked, 'What happening now?'

Hat said, 'Is about Big Foot.'

Boyee said, 'What, they throw him in jail again?'

Hat said, 'Big Foot taking up boxing.'

I understood more than I could say.

Hat said, 'He go get his tail mash up. If he think that boxing is just throwing yourself around, he go find out his mistake.'

The newspapers made a big thing out of it The most popular headline was *Prankster Turns Pugilist.*

And when I next saw Big Foot, I felt I could look him in the eyes.

And now I wasn't afraid of him, I was afraid for him.

But I had no need. Big Foot had what the sports-writers all called a 'phenomenal success'. He knocked out fighter after fighter, and Miguel Street grew more afraid of him and more proud of him.

Hat said, 'Is only because he only fighting stupid little people. He ain't meet anybody yet that have real class.'

Big Foot seemed to have forgotten me. His eyes no longer sought mine whenever we met, and he no longer stopped to talk to me.

He was the terror of the street. I, like everybody else, was frightened of him. As before, I preferred it that way.

He even began showing off more.

We used to see him running up and down Miguel Street in stupid-looking maroon shorts and he resolutely refused to notice anybody.

Hat was terrified.

He said, 'They shouldn't let a man who go to jail box.'

An Englishman came to Trinidad one day and the papers ran to interview him. The man said he was a boxer and a champion of the Royal Air Force. Next morning his picture appeared.

Two days later another picture of him appeared. This time he was dressed only in black shorts, and he had squared up towards the cameraman with his boxing gloves on.

The headline said, '*Who will fight this man?*'

And Trinidad answered, 'Big Foot will fight this man.'

The excitement was intense when Big Foot agreed. Miguel Street was in the news, and even Hat was pleased.

Hat said, 'I know is stupid to say, but I hope Big Foot beat him.' And he went around the district placing bets with everyone who had money to throw away.

We turned up in strength at the stadium on the night.

Hat rushed madly here and there, waving a twenty-dollar bill, shouting, 'Twenty to five, Big Foot beat him.'

I bet Boyee six cents that Big Foot would lose.

And, in truth, when Big Foot came out to the ring, dancing disdainfully in the ring, without looking at anybody in the crowd, we felt pleased.

Hat shouted, 'That is man!'

I couldn't bear to look at the fight. I looked all the time at the only woman in the crowd. She was an American or a Canadian woman and she was nibbling at peanuts. She was so blonde, her hair looked like straw. Whenever a blow was landed, the crowd roared, and the woman pulled in her lips as though she had given the blow, and then she nibbled furiously at her peanuts. She never shouted or got up or waved her hands. I hated that woman.

The roars grew louder and more frequent.

I could hear Hat shouting, 'Come on, Big Foot. Beat him up. Beat him up, man.' Then, with panic in his voice, 'Remember your father.'

But Hat's shouts died away.

Big Foot had lost the fight, on points.

Hat paid out about a hundred dollars in five minutes.

He said, 'I go have to sell the brown and white cow, the one I buy from George.'

Edward said, 'Is God work.'

Boyee said to me, 'I go give you your six cents tomorrow.'

I said, 'Six cents *tomorrow*? But what you think I is? A millionaire? Look, man, give me money now now, you hear.'

He paid up.

But the crowd was laughing, laughing.

I looked at the ring.

Big Foot was in tears. He was like a boy, and the more he cried, the louder he cried, and the more painful it sounded.

The secret I had held for Big Foot was now shown to everybody.

Hat said, 'What, he crying?' And Hat laughed.

He seemed to forget all about the cow. He said, 'Well, well, look at man, eh!'

And all of us from Miguel Street laughed at Big Foot.

All except me. For I knew how he felt although he was a big man and I was a boy. I wished I had never betted that six cents with Boyee.

The papers next morning said, 'PUGILIST SOBS IN RING.'

Trinidad thought it was Big Foot, the comedian, doing something funny again.

But we knew otherwise.

Big Foot left Miguel Street, and the last I heard of him was that he was a labourer in a quarry in Laventille.

About six months later a little scandal was rippling through Trinidad, making everybody feel silly.

The R.A.F. champion, it turned out, had never been in the R.A.F., and as a boxer he was completely unknown.

Hat said, 'Well, what you expect in a place like this?'

NOTES

good good (p54)
   (*Trinidadian slang*) very good or well (repeating the word has the
   same effect as saying 'very')
beating his pans (p55)
   players in a steel band make music by beating the surface of the drum
   – the pan – with a stick
working a small racket (p56)
   (*slang*) organizing a dishonest or illegal way to make some money
Joe (p57)
   (*US slang*) a name used when speaking to someone whose name you
   don't know
fraid (p57)
   (be) afraid of
to come friendly (p58)
   to be friends
his feet were not big for nothing (p58)
   it proved useful that he had big feet

DISCUSSION

1   What exactly is Big Foot's secret, and what does he do to try and hide
    it? Why is he successful? Would you describe it as cowardice?

2   Big Foot's father features quite prominently in the story. Why do you
    think this is so? What effect do you think his father had on him?

3   The incident with the American soldier, the incident with the dog, and
    the fight with the R.A.F. champion all reveal something about Big
    Foot. What does each one reveal?

4   What twist does the final paragraph add to the story? How does it
    relate to the incident with the dog?

5   Apart from Big Foot, the narrator and Hat also figure prominently in
    this story, and we see him very much through their eyes. How would
    you describe their characters?

6   The story takes place in the particular setting of Trinidad and at a
    particular time. Do you think this reduces the more general relevance
    of the theme it deals with?

LANGUAGE FOCUS

1 Find these expressions in the story and rewrite them in simple English.

- '*How you does let people give you stupidness like that?*' (p56)
- '*. . . is a good thing Big Foot father dead before Big Foot really get big.*' (p57)
- '*But I feel you do him something and you worried.*' (p57)
- '*. . . then we all want to come friendly with him. But he don't want we at all at all.*' (p58)
- '*Like Big Foot have something with you, boy.*' (p60)

2 Naipaul has written the narrative part of the story in Standard English and the dialogue in Trinidadian dialect. Do you think this works? Is it easy enough to understand the dialogue sections? Would it be better if it were written entirely in Standard English or entirely in dialect?

3 Having read the story, what significance do you think the following quotations have for understanding Big Foot's character?

- *Big Foot was always ready to start a fight with another band, but he looked so big and dangerous that he himself was never involved in any fight.* (p55)
- *He began hugging and stroking the wet dog, and laughing in a crazy way.* (p59)
- *I knew how he felt although he was a big man and I was a boy.* (p63)

ACTIVITIES

1 Write the article that might have appeared under the headline 'Prankster Turns Pugilist', or the later headline 'Pugilist Sobs in Ring'.

2 Is *The Coward* a good title for this story? Why do you think the author chose it? Would any of these titles be more, or less, appropriate? Why?

> *The Fall of Big Foot*   *The Little Boy Inside Big Foot*
> *A Dangerous Secret*   *Big Foot in Hiding*

Now think of a few more titles of your own, and explain why they would be appropriate to the story.

3 Once the news about Big Foot's opponent is out, suppose the narrator and Hat are discussing Big Foot. Write the conversation between them in which the narrator reveals Big Foot's secret.

Mr Know-All

The Author

William Somerset Maugham was born in 1874. He originally qualified as a surgeon but soon became a full-time writer of plays, short stories, and novels. In both world wars he served as a British Intelligence agent, and travelled widely in the South Seas, south-east Asia, China, and Mexico. Many of his experiences in these places were later incorporated into his stories. His most famous novels are *Of Human Bondage, The Moon and Sixpence, Cakes and Ale,* and *The Razor's Edge*. His short stories have been published in various collections, and include some that have been considered among the best in the language, such as 'Rain' and 'The Alien Corn'. Many have been made into films or plays for the theatre. Maugham died in 1965.

The Story

Travelling in the company of strangers can be a delight or a disaster. The chatty passenger in the next seat may help to while away an hour or two, but would you find the conversation so entertaining after a day – or a week? How much worse, then, if your companion is eager, sociable, thick-skinned, and knows everything, and you are doomed to be together for a fortnight.

Mr Kelada is just such a person. He is an authority on every subject, never forgets a name, and cannot imagine the possibility that he is not wanted. How can the other passengers tolerate him? And is there anything in the world that could possibly be more important to Mr Kelada than being right and having the last word?

Mr Know-All

I was prepared to dislike Max Kelada even before I knew him. The war* had just finished and the passenger traffic in the ocean-going liners was heavy. Accommodation was very hard to get and you had to put up with whatever the agents chose to offer you. You could not hope for a cabin to yourself and I was thankful to be given one in which there were only two berths. But when I was told the name of my companion my heart sank. It suggested closed port-holes and the night air rigidly excluded. It was bad enough to share a cabin for fourteen days with anyone (I was going from San Francisco to Yokohama), but I should have looked upon it with less dismay if my fellow passenger's name had been Smith or Brown.

When I went on board I found Mr Kelada's luggage already below. I did not like the look of it; there were too many labels on the suitcases, and the wardrobe trunk was too big. He had unpacked his toilet things, and I observed that he was a patron of the excellent Monsieur Coty*; for I saw on the washing-stand his scent, his hair-wash, and his brilliantine. Mr Kelada's brushes, ebony with his monogram in gold, would have been all the better for a scrub. I did not at all like Mr Kelada. I made my way into the smoking-room. I called for a pack of cards and began to play patience. I had scarcely started before a man came up to me and asked me if he was right in thinking my name was so-and-so.

'I am Mr Kelada,' he added, with a smile that showed a row of flashing teeth, and sat down.

'Oh, yes, we're sharing a cabin, I think.'

'Bit of luck, I call it. You never know who you're going to be put in with. I was jolly glad when I heard you were English. I'm all for us English sticking together when we're abroad, if you understand what I mean.'

I blinked.

'Are you English?' I asked, perhaps tactlessly.

'Rather. You don't think I look an American, do you? British to the backbone, that's what I am.'

To prove it, Mr Kelada took out of his pocket a passport and airily waved it under my nose.

King George* has many strange subjects. Mr Kelada was short and of a sturdy build, clean-shaven and dark-skinned, with a fleshy, hooked nose and very large, lustrous and liquid eyes. His long black hair was sleek and curly. He spoke with a fluency in which there was nothing English and his gestures were exuberant. I felt pretty sure that a closer inspection of that British passport would have betrayed the fact that Mr Kelada was born under a bluer sky than is generally seen in England.

'What will you have?' he asked me.

I looked at him doubtfully. Prohibition* was in force and to all appearances the ship was bone-dry*. When I am not thirsty I do not know which I dislike more, ginger-ale or lemon-squash. But Mr Kelada flashed an oriental smile at me.

'Whisky and soda or a dry Martini, you have only to say the word.'

From each of his hip-pockets he fished a flask and laid them on the table before me. I chose the Martini, and calling the steward he ordered a tumbler of ice and a couple of glasses.

'A very good cocktail,' I said.

'Well, there are plenty more where that came from, and if you've got any friends on board, you tell them you've got a pal who's got all the liquor in the world.'

Mr Kelada was chatty. He talked of New York and of San Francisco. He discussed plays, pictures, and politics. He was patriotic. The Union Jack is an impressive piece of drapery, but when it is flourished by a gentleman from Alexandria or Beirut, I cannot but feel that it loses somewhat in dignity. Mr Kelada was familiar. I do not wish to put on airs, but I cannot help feeling that it is seemly in a total stranger to put mister before my name when he addresses me. Mr Kelada, doubtless to set me at my ease, used no such formality. I did not like Mr Kelada. I had put aside the cards when he sat down, but now, thinking that for this first occasion our conversation had lasted long enough, I went on with my game.

'The three on the four,' said Mr Kelada.

There is nothing more exasperating when you are playing patience than to be told where to put the card you have turned up before you have had a chance to look for yourself.

'It's coming out, it's coming out,' he cried. 'The ten on the knave.'

With rage and hatred in my heart I finished. Then he seized the pack.

'Do you like card tricks?'

'No, I hate card tricks,' I answered.

'Well, I'll just show you this one.'

He showed me three. Then I said I would go down to the dining-room and get my seat at table.

'Oh, that's all right,' he said. 'I've already taken a seat for you. I thought that as we were in the same state-room we might just as well sit at the same table.'

I did not like Mr Kelada.

I not only shared a cabin with him and ate three meals a day at the same table, but I could not walk round the deck without his joining me. It was impossible to snub him. It never occurred to him that he was not wanted. He was certain that you were as glad to see him as he was to see you. In your own house you might have kicked him downstairs and slammed the door in his face without the suspicion dawning on him that he was not a welcome visitor.

He was a good mixer, and in three days knew everyone on board. He ran everything. He managed the sweeps*, conducted the auctions, collected money for prizes at the sports, got up quoit and golf matches, organized the concert, and arranged the fancy-dress ball. He was everywhere and always. He was certainly the best-hated man in the ship. We called him Mr Know-All, even to his face. He took it as a compliment. But it was at meal times that he was most intolerable. For the better part of an hour then he had us at his mercy. He was hearty, jovial, loquacious and argumentative. He knew everything better than anybody else, and it was an affront to his overweening vanity that you should disagree with him. He would not drop a subject, however unimportant, till he had brought you round to his way of thinking. The possibility that he could be mistaken never occurred to him. He was the chap who knew. We sat at the doctor's table. Mr Kelada would certainly have had it all his own way, for the doctor was lazy and I was frigidly indifferent, except for a man called Ramsay who sat there also. He was as dogmatic as Mr Kelada and resented bitterly the Levantine's* cocksureness. The discussions they had were acrimonious and interminable.

Ramsay was in the American Consular Service, and was stationed at Kobe. He was a great heavy fellow from the Middle West, with loose fat under a tight skin, and he bulged out of his ready-made clothes. He was on his way back to resume his post, having been on a flying visit to New York to fetch his wife, who had been spending a year at home. Mrs Ramsay was a very pretty little thing, with pleasant manners and a sense of humour. The Consular Service is ill paid, and she was dressed always very simply; but she knew how to wear her clothes. She achieved an effect of quiet distinction. I should not have paid any particular attention to her but that she possessed a quality that may be common enough in women, but nowadays is not obvious in their demeanour. You could not look at her without being struck by her modesty. It shone in her like a flower on a coat.

One evening at dinner the conversation by chance drifted to the subject of pearls. There had been in the papers a good deal of talk about the culture pearls* which the cunning Japanese were making, and the doctor remarked that they must inevitably diminish the value of real ones. They were very good already; they would soon be perfect. Mr Kelada, as was his habit, rushed the new topic. He told us all that was to be known about pearls. I do not believe Ramsay knew anything about them at all, but he could not resist the opportunity to have a fling* at the Levantine, and in five minutes we were in the middle of a heated argument. I had seen Mr Kelada vehement and voluble before, but never so voluble and vehement as now. At last something that Ramsay said stung him, for he thumped the table and shouted:

'Well, I ought to know what I am talking about. I'm going to Japan just to look into this Japanese pearl business. I'm in the trade and there's not a man in it who won't tell you that what I say about pearls goes. I know all the best pearls in the world, and what I don't know about pearls isn't worth knowing.'

Here was news for us, for Mr Kelada, with all his loquacity, had never told anyone what his business was. We only knew vaguely that he was going to Japan on some commercial errand. He looked round the table triumphantly.

'They'll never be able to get a culture pearl that an expert like me can't tell with half an eye.' He pointed to a chain that Mrs Ramsay wore. 'You take my word for it, Mrs Ramsay, that chain you're wearing will never be worth a cent less than it is now.'

Mrs Ramsay in her modest way flushed a little and slipped the chain inside her dress. Ramsay leaned forward. He gave us all a look and a smile flickered in his eyes.

'That's a pretty chain of Mrs Ramsay's, isn't it?'

'I noticed it at once,' answered Mr Kelada. 'Gee, I said to myself, those are pearls all right.'

'I didn't buy it myself, of course. I'd be interested to know how much you think it cost.'

'Oh, in the trade somewhere round fifteen thousand dollars. But if it was bought on Fifth Avenue* I shouldn't be surprised to hear that anything up to thirty thousand was paid for it.'

Ramsay smiled grimly.

'You'll be surprised to hear that Mrs Ramsay bought that string at a department store the day before we left New York, for eighteen dollars.'

Mr Kelada flushed.

'Rot. It's not only real, but it's as fine a string for its size as I've ever seen.'

'Will you bet on it? I'll bet you a hundred dollars it's imitation.'

'Done.'

'Oh, Elmer, you can't bet on a certainty,' said Mrs Ramsay.

She had a little smile on her lips and her tone was gently deprecating.

'Can't I? If I get a chance of easy money like that I should be all sorts of a fool not to take it.'

'But how can it be proved?' she continued. 'It's only my word against Mr Kelada's.'

'Let me look at the chain, and if it's imitation I'll tell you quickly enough. I can afford to lose a hundred dollars,' said Mr Kelada.

'Take it off, dear. Let the gentleman look at it as much as he wants.'

Mrs Ramsay hesitated a moment. She put her hands to the clasp.

'I can't undo it,' she said. 'Mr Kelada will just have to take my word for it.'

I had a sudden suspicion that something unfortunate was about to occur, but I could think of nothing to say.

Ramsay jumped up.

'I'll undo it.'

He handed the chain to Mr Kelada. The Levantine took a magnifying glass from his pocket and closely examined it. A smile of triumph spread over his smooth and swarthy face. He handed back the chain. He was about to speak. Suddenly he caught sight of Mrs Ramsay's face. It was so white that she looked as though she were about to faint. She was staring at him with wide and terrified eyes. They held a desperate appeal; it was so clear that I wondered why her husband did not see it.

Mr Kelada stopped with his mouth open. He flushed deeply. You could almost *see* the effort he was making over himself.

'I was mistaken,' he said. 'It's a very good imitation, but of course as soon as I looked through my glass I saw that it wasn't real. I think eighteen dollars is just about as much as the damned thing's worth.'

He took out his pocket-book and from it a hundred-dollar note. He handed it to Ramsay without a word.

'Perhaps that'll teach you not to be so cocksure another time, my young friend,' said Ramsay as he took the note.

I noticed that Mr Kelada's hands were trembling.

The story spread over the ship as stories do, and he had to put up with a good deal of chaff* that evening. It was a fine joke that Mr Know-All had been caught out. But Mrs Ramsay retired to her state-room with a headache.

Next morning I got up and began to shave. Mr Kelada lay on his bed smoking a cigarette. Suddenly there was a small scraping sound and I saw a letter pushed under the door. I opened the door and looked out. There was nobody there. I picked up the letter and saw that it was addressed to Max Kelada. The name was written in block letters. I handed it to him.

'Who's this from?' He opened it. 'Oh!'

He took out of the envelope, not a letter, but a hundred-dollar note. He looked at me and again he reddened. He tore the envelope into little bits and gave them to me.

'Do you mind just throwing them out of the port-hole?'

I did as he asked, and then I looked at him with a smile. 'No one likes being made to look a perfect damned fool,' he said.

'Were the pearls real?'

'If I had a pretty little wife I shouldn't let her spend a year in New York while I stayed at Kobe,' said he.

At that moment I did not entirely dislike Mr Kelada. He reached out for his pocket-book and carefully put in it the hundred-dollar note.

NOTES

The war (p67)
  the First World War (1914–18)
Monsieur Coty (p67)
  a well-known brand of toiletries
King George (p68)
  George V (1865–1936), king of the United Kingdom 1910–36
Prohibition (p68)
  the period from 1920 to 1933 when the making and selling of
  alcoholic drinks was illegal in the United States
bone-dry (p68)
  (here) entirely without alcohol
the sweeps (p70)
  sweepstake – a betting game in which the winner gets all the money
Levantine (p70)
  a person from the eastern part of the Mediterranean
culture pearl (p71)
  (more usually) cultured pearl – a pearl that is created artificially
have a fling at someone (p71)
  challenge somebody's authority
Fifth Avenue (p72)
  an expensive shopping street in New York
chaff (p73)
  teasing

DISCUSSION

1 What kind of person is the narrator? Compare his character with that
   of Mr Kelada. What evidence do you find that the narrator is inclined
   to dislike Mr Kelada even before he has met him? What is it that causes
   this dislike? What kind of attitude does this reveal?

2 Given Mr Kelada's love of being right and winning the argument, why
   do you think he lied to Mr Ramsay? Do you think he was right to lie in
   this way? Why?

3 Who do you think the hundred-dollar note came from – Mr Ramsay,
   or Mrs Ramsay? If it was Mrs Ramsay, what message is she sending to
   Mr Kelada? If it was Mr Ramsay, why has he given it back?

LANGUAGE FOCUS

1   The way the narrator expresses himself is often quite oblique and
    complicated. Explain these expressions from the text in simple
    English.

    • *. . . a closer inspection of that British passport would have
      betrayed the fact that Mr Kelada was born under a bluer sky than
      is generally seen in England.* (p68)

    • *I do not wish to put on airs, but I cannot help feeling that it is
      seemly in a total stranger to put mister before my name when he
      addresses me.* (p69)

    • *I should not have paid any particular attention to her but that she
      possessed a quality that may be common enough in women, but
      nowadays is not obvious in their demeanour.* (p70)

2   *I did not like Mr Kelada.*
    At what points in the story is this sentence repeated? What is the effect
    of this, and how is it altered by the last sentence but one in the story?

3   Consider the paragraph which begins *King George has many strange
    subjects* (p68). What does this description reveal about the narrator?

4   *I noticed that Mr Kelada's hands were trembling* (p73)
    What do you suppose might be the reason for this?

ACTIVITIES

1   Somebody bought the string of pearls and gave them to Mrs Ramsay.
    Write a letter in which she tells this person the events on board ship
    concerning the necklace.

2   What passes between Mr and Mrs Ramsay that night? How much – if
    any – of the truth does she tell him? Write the conversation between
    them when they return to the cabin.

3   Imagine that after disembarkation at Yokohama, Mr Kelada explains
    himself more fully to the narrator. Write down what he says. How does
    he explain the choices that were available to him and the consequences
    as he saw them? You might begin like this:

    *My friend, I saw at once that those pearls were real – and very
    valuable. But what could I say? If I said . . .*

SHARP PRACTICE

THE AUTHOR

Frederick Forsyth was born in Ashford, Kent, in 1938. At nineteen he became the youngest pilot in the Royal Air Force. He later left to become a journalist and worked in Paris and then in East Germany, where his experiences provided him with material which he was to use in his thrillers. His first success was with *The Day of the Jackal* in 1970, and he went on to write another eight bestsellers, including *The Odessa File*, *The Dogs of War*, and *The Fourth Protocol*. These nine titles sold fifty million copies in more than thirty languages, and five of them were filmed. His novels are noted for their factual accuracy, high tension, and driving pace. Recently Forsyth has begun publishing his short stories as e-books on the Internet.

THE STORY

Cheating people out of their money is wrong – of course it is. Even so, it is hard not to feel a sneaking admiration for a plan that shows real cunning and daring. Naturally the victim attracts our sympathy – but if the victim has plenty of money in any case, our sympathy is a little less. And if the victim finds the experience entertaining, and has even been the one to begin the activity that leads to his being cheated – well, they can hardly expect many tears.

On the slow train from Dublin to Tralee, Judge Comyn plans to pass the time dealing with his paperwork. He is not alone in the compartment, but fortunately the other passengers are quiet. The little sandy-haired man has begun a game of patience, but seems very inexpert at it. Can't he see that the red nine should go on the black ten? Judge Comyn finds it hard to resist intervening . . .

SHARP PRACTICE

Judge Comyn settled himself comfortably into the corner seat of his first-class compartment, unfolded his day's copy of the *Irish Times*, glanced at the headlines, and laid it on his lap.

There would be plenty of time for the newspaper during the slow four-hour trundle down to Tralee. He gazed idly out of the window at the bustle of Kingsbridge station in the last minutes before the departure of the Dublin-Tralee locomotive which would haul him sedately to his duties in the principal township of County Kerry. He hoped vaguely he would have the compartment to himself so that he could deal with his paperwork.

It was not to be. Hardly had the thought crossed his mind when the compartment door opened and someone stepped in. He forbore to look. The door rolled shut and the newcomer tossed a handgrip onto the luggage rack. Then the man sat down opposite him, across the gleaming walnut table.

Judge Comyn gave him a glance. His companion was a small, wispy man, with a puckish quiff of sandy hair standing up from his forehead and a pair of the saddest, most apologetic brown eyes. His suit was of a whiskery thornproof* with a matching weskit* and knitted tie. The judge assessed him as someone associated with horses, or a clerk perhaps, and resumed his gaze out of the window.

He heard the call of the guard outside to the driver of the old steam engine puffing away somewhere down the line, and then the shrill blast of the guard's whistle. Even as the engine emitted its first great chuff and the carriage began to lurch forward, a large running figure dressed entirely in black scurried past the window. The judge heard the crash of the carriage door opening a few feet away and the thud of a body landing in the corridor. Seconds later, to the accompaniment of a wheezing and puffing, the black figure appeared in the compartment's doorway and subsided with relief into the far corner.

Judge Comyn glanced again. The newcomer was a florid-faced priest. The judge looked again out of the window; he did not wish to start a conversation, having been schooled in England.

'By the saints, ye nearly didn't make it, Father,' he heard the wispy one say.

There was more puffing from the man of the cloth. 'It was a sight too close for comfort, my son,' the priest replied.

After that they mercifully lapsed into silence. Judge Comyn observed Kingsbridge station slide out of sight, to be replaced by the unedifying rows of smoke-grimed houses that in those days made up the western suburbs of Dublin. The loco of the Great Southern Railway Company took the strain and the clickety-clack tempo of the wheels over the rails increased. Judge Comyn picked up his paper.

The headline and leading news item concerned the premier, Eamon de Valera*, who the previous day in the Dail* had given his full support to his agriculture minister in the matter of the price of potatoes. Far down at the bottom was a two-inch mention that a certain Mr Hitler had taken over Austria. The editor was a man who had his priorities right, thought Judge Comyn. There was little more to interest him in the paper, and after five minutes he folded it, took a batch of legal papers from his briefcase and began to peruse them. The green fields of Kildare slid by the windows soon after they cleared the city of Dublin.

'Sir,' said a timid voice from opposite him. Oh dear, he thought, he wants to talk. He raised his gaze to the pleading spaniel eyes of the man opposite.

'Would you mind if I used a part of the table?' asked the man.

'Not at all,' said the judge.

'Thank you sir,' said the man, with a detectable brogue from the southwest of the country.

The judge resumed his study of the papers relating to the settlement of a complex civil issue he would have to adjudicate on his return to Dublin from Tralee. The visit to Kerry as circuit court judge to preside over the quarterly hearings there would, he trusted, offer no such complexities. These rural circuit courts, in his experience, offered only the simplest of issues to be decided by local juries who as often as not produced verdicts of bewildering illogicality.

He did not bother to look up when the wispy man produced a pack of none-too-clean playing cards from his pockets and proceeded to set some of them out in columns to play patience. His attention was only drawn some seconds later to a clucking sound. He looked up again.

The wispy man had his tongue between his teeth in an effort of great concentration – this was producing the clucking sound – and was staring at the exposed cards at the foot of each column. Judge Comyn observed at a glance that a red nine had not been placed upon a black ten, even though both cards were clearly visible. The wispy man, failing to see the match, began to deal three more cards. Judge Comyn choked back his irritation and returned to his papers. Nothing to do with me, he told himself.

But there is something mesmeric about a man playing patience, and never more so than when he is playing it badly. Within five minutes the judge's concentration had been completely broken in the matter of the civil lawsuit, and he was staring at the exposed cards. Finally he could bear it no longer. There was an empty column on the right, yet an exposed king on column three that ought to go into the vacant space. He coughed. The wispy one looked up in alarm.

'The king,' said the judge gently, 'it should go up into the space.'

The cardplayer looked down, spotted the opportunity and moved the king. The card now able to be turned over proved to be a queen, and she went to the king. Before he had finished he had legitimately made seven moves. The column that began with the king now ended with a ten.

'And the red nine,' said the judge. 'It can go across now.'

The red nine and its dependent six cards moved over to the ten. Another card could be exposed; an ace, which went up above the game.

'I do believe you will get it out,' said the judge.

'Ah, not me, sir,' said the wispy man, shaking his head with its sad spaniel eyes. 'Sure I've never got one out yet in all me life.'

'Play on, play on,' said Judge Comyn with rising interest. With his help the game did indeed come out. The wispy man gazed at the resolved puzzle in wonderment.

'There you are, you see; you've done it,' said the judge.

'Ah, but not without your honour's help,' said the sad-eyed one. 'It's a fine mind ye have for the cards, sir.'

Judge Comyn wondered if the cardplayer could possibly know he was a judge, but concluded the man was simply using a common form of address in Ireland in those days towards one worthy of some respect.

Even the priest had laid down his collection of the sermons of the late, great Cardinal Newman* and was looking at the cards.

'Oh,' said the judge, who played a little bridge and poker with his cronies at the Kildare Street Club, 'not really.'

Privately he was rather proud of his theory that a good legal mind, with its trained observation, practised powers of deduction and keen memory, could always play a good game of cards.

The wispy man ceased playing and began idly dealing five-card hands, which he then examined before returning the cards to the pack. Finally he put the deck down. He sighed.

'It's a long way to Tralee,' he said wistfully.

With hindsight Judge Comyn never could recall who exactly had mentioned the word poker, but he suspected it might have been himself. Anyway, he took over the pack and dealt a few hands for himself. One of them, he was pleased to notice, was a full house, jacks on tens.

With a half-smile, as if amazed at his boldness, the wispy man took up one hand and held it in front of him.

'I will bet you, sir, one imaginary penny that you cannot deal yourself a better hand than this one.'

'Done,' said the judge, and dealt a second hand, which he held up in front of him. It was not a full house, but contained a pair of nines.

'Ready?' asked Judge Comyn. The wispy man nodded. They put their cards down. The wispy man had three fives.

'Ah,' said the judge, 'but I did not draw any fresh cards, as was my right. Again, my dear fellow.'

They did it again. This time the wispy man drew three fresh cards, the judge two. The judge had the better hand.

'I win my imaginary penny back,' said the judge.

'That you do, sir,' said the other. 'That was a fine hand. You have the knack of the cards. I have seen it, though not having it myself. Yes, sir. The knack it is.'

'Nothing but clear deduction and the calculated risk,' corrected Judge Comyn.

At this point they exchanged names, only surnames as was the practice in those days. The judge omitted his title, giving his name simply as Comyn, and the other revealed he was O'Connor. Five minutes later, between Sallins and Kildare, they attempted a little friendly poker. Five-card draw seemed the appropriate form and went without saying. There was, of course, no money involved.

'The trouble is,' said O'Connor after the third hand, 'I cannot remember who has wagered what. Your honour has his fine memory to help him.'

'I have it,' said Judge Comyn, and triumphantly foraged in his briefcase for a large box of matches. He enjoyed a cigar after his breakfast and another after dinner, and would never have used a petrol lighter on a good fourpenny Havana*.

''Tis the very thing,' said O'Connor in wonderment as the judge dealt out twenty matchsticks each.

They played a dozen hands, with some enjoyment, and honours were about even. But it is hard to play two-handed poker, for if one party, having a poor hand, wants to 'fold*', the other party is finished also. Just past Kildare town O'Connor asked the priest, 'Father, would you not care to join us?'

'Oh, I fear not,' said the rubicund priest with a laugh, 'for I am no hand with the cards. Though,' he added, 'I did once play a little whist with the lads in the seminary.'

'It's the same principle, Father,' said the judge. 'Once learned, never forgotten. You are simply dealt a hand of five cards; you can draw fresh ones up to five if you are not happy with the deal. Then you assess whether the hand you hold is good or bad. If it is good, you wager it is better than ours, if not, you decline to wager, and fold your hand.'

'I'm not certain about wagering,' said the priest doubtfully.

''Tis only matchsticks, Father,' said O'Connor.

'Does one try to take tricks?' asked the priest.

O'Connor raised his eyebrows. Judge Comyn laughed a trifle patronizingly.

'No taking of tricks,' he said. 'The hand you hold is evaluated according to a precise scale of values. Look . . .'

He rummaged in his briefcase and produced a sheet of white lined paper. From his inner pocket a rolled-gold propelling pencil. He began to write on the sheet. The priest peered to see.

'Top of the list,' said the judge, 'is the royal flush. That means five cards, all in the same suit, all in sequence and beginning with the ace. Since they must be in sequence that means, of course, that the others must be king, queen, jack and ten.'

'I suppose so,' said the priest warily.

'Then comes four of a kind,' said the judge, writing the words in below the royal flush. 'That means exactly what it says. Four aces, four kings, four queens and so forth down to four twos. Never mind the fifth card. And, of course, four aces is better than four kings or anything else. All right?'

The priest nodded.

'Then comes the full house,' said O'Connor.

'Not quite,' corrected Judge Comyn. 'The straight flush comes next, my friend.'

O'Connor clapped his forehead in the manner of one who admits he is a fool. 'Of course, that's true,' he said. 'You see, Father, the straight flush is like the royal, save only that it is not led off by an ace. But the five cards must be of the same suit and in sequence.'

The judge wrote his description under the words 'four of a kind' on the sheet of paper.

'Now comes Mr O'Connor's full house, which means three of a kind and two of another kind, making up the full five cards. If the three cards are tens and the other two queens, this is called a full house, tens on queens.'

The priest nodded again.

The judge went down the list, explaining each hand, through 'flush', 'straight', 'threes', 'two pairs', 'one pair' and 'ace high*'.

'Now,' he said when he had finished, 'obviously one pair, or ace high, or a mixed hand, which is called a bag of nails, would be so poor you really wouldn't wager on them.'

The father gazed at the list. 'Could I refer to this?' he asked.

'Of course,' said Judge Comyn, 'keep it by you, Father, by all means.'

'Well, seeing as it's only for matchsticks . . .' said the priest, and was dealt in. Friendly games of chance, after all, are not a sin. Not for matchsticks. They divided the sticks into three even piles and began to play.

For the first two hands the priest folded early, watching the others bid. The judge won four matchsticks. On the third hand the priest's face lit up.

'Is that not good?' he asked, displaying his hand to the other two. It *was* good; a full house, jacks on kings. The judge folded his own hand in exasperation.

'Yes, it's very good, Father,' said O'Connor patiently, 'but you are not supposed to show us, don't you see? For if we know what you have, we will not wager anything if our hand is not as good as yours. Your own hand should be . . . well now, like the confessional*.'

That made sense to the priest. 'Like the confessional,' he repeated. 'Yes, I see. Not a word to anyone, eh?'

He apologized and they started again. For sixty minutes up to Thurles they played fifteen hands, and the judge's pile of matchsticks mounted. The priest was almost cleaned out and sad-eyed O'Connor had only half his pile left. He made too many lapses; the good father seemed half at sea; only the judge played hard, calculating poker, assessing the options and odds with his legally trained mind. The game was a vindication of his theory of mind over luck. Just after Thurles O'Connor's mind seemed to wander. The judge had to call him to the game twice.

'I fear it's not very interesting, playing with matchsticks,' he confessed after the second time. 'Shall we not end it here?'

'Oh, I confess I'm rather enjoying it,' said the judge. Most winners enjoy the game.

'Or we could make it more interesting,' said O'Connor apologetically. 'I'm not by nature a betting man, but a few shillings would do no harm.'

'If you wish,' said the judge, 'though I observe that you have lost a few matches.'

'Ah, your honour, my luck must change soon,' said O'Connor with his elfin smile.

'Then I must retire,' said the priest with finality. 'For I fear I have but three pounds in my purse, and that to last me through my holiday with my mother at Dingle.'

'But, Father,' said O'Connor, 'without you we could not play. And a few shillings . . .'

'Even a few shillings, my son, are too much for me,' said the priest. 'The Holy Mother Church is no place for men who want to have money jingling in their pockets.'

'Wait,' said the judge, 'I have it. You and I, O'Connor, will divide the matchsticks between us. We will each then lend the good Father an equal amount of sticks, the sticks by now having a value. If he loses, we will not claim our debt. If he wins, he will repay us the sticks we loaned him, and benefit by the balance.'

''Tis a genius you are, your honour,' said O'Connor in wonderment.

'But I could not gamble for money,' protested the priest.

There was a gloomy silence for a while.

'Unless any winnings went to a Church charity?' suggested O'Connor. 'Surely the Lord would not object to that?'

'It's the Bishop who would object,' said the priest, 'and I may well meet him first. Still . . . there *is* the orphanage at Dingle. My mother prepares the meals there, and the poor wains* are fierce cold in winter, with the price of turf being what it is . . .'

'A donation,' cried the judge in triumph. He turned to his bewildered companions. 'Anything the father wins, over and above the stake we lend him, is our joint donation to the orphanage. What do you say?'

'I suppose even our Bishop could not object to a donation to the orphanage . . .' said the priest.

'And the donation will be our gift in return for your company at a game of cards,' said O'Connor. ''Tis perfect.'

The priest agreed and they started again. The judge and O'Connor split the sticks into two piles. O'Connor pointed out that with under fifty sticks they might run out of tokens. Judge Comyn solved that one too. They broke the sticks in halves; those halves with a sulphur head were worth twice those without.

O'Connor averred that he was carrying his personal holiday money of over £30 on him, and to this limit would play the game. There was no question of either party refusing Comyn's cheque; he was so obviously a gentleman.

This done, they loaned the priest ten matches with heads and four without, half from each of them.

'Now,' said Judge Comyn as he shuffled the cards, 'what about the stakes?'

O'Connor held up half a matchstick without any head on it.

'Ten shillings?' he said. That shook the judge a bit. The forty matchsticks he had emptied from his box were now in eighty halves, representing £60 sterling, a sizable sum in 1938. The priest had £12 in front of him, the other two men £24 each at those values. He heard the priest sigh.

'In for a penny, in for a pound. Lord help me,' said the priest.

The judge nodded abruptly. He need not have worried. He took the first two hands and nearly £10 with it. In the third hand O'Connor folded early, losing his 10s. playing stake yet again. The priest put down four of his £1 matchsticks. Judge Comyn looked at his hand; he had a full house, jacks on sevens. It had to be better. The priest only had £7 left.

'I'll cover your four pounds, Father,' he said pushing his matches to the centre, 'and I'll raise you five pounds.'

'Oh dear,' he said, 'I'm nearly out. What can I do?'

'Only one thing,' said O'Connor, 'if you don't want Mr Comyn to raise you again to a sum you cannot cover. Push five pounds forward and ask to see the cards.'

'I'll see the cards,' said the priest, as if reciting a ritual as he pushed five headed matchsticks forward. The judge put down his full house and waited. The priest laid out four tens. He got his £9 back, plus another £9 from the judge, plus the 30s. table stakes. With his £2 still in hand, he had £21 10s.

In this manner they arrived at Limerick Junction which, as is proper for an Irish railway system, is nowhere near Limerick but just outside Tipperary. Here the train went past the main platform, then backed up to it, since the platform could not be reached on the down line. A few people got on and off, but no one disturbed the game or entered the compartment.

By Charleville the priest had taken £10 off O'Connor, who was looking worried, and the game slowed up. O'Connor tended to fold quickly, and too many hands ended with another player electing to fold as well. Just before Mallow, by agreement, they eliminated all the small cards, keeping sevens and up, and making a thirty-two-card deck. Then the game speeded up again.

By Headford poor O'Connor was down £12 and the judge £20, both to the priest.

'Would it not be a good idea if I paid back now the twelve pounds I started with?' asked the priest.

Both the others agreed it would. They got their £6 loans back. The priest still had £32 to play with. O'Connor continued to play cautiously, only wagering high and winning £10 back with a full house that beat two pairs and a flush. The lakes of Killarney drifted by the window unadmired.

Out of Farranfore the judge knew he had the hand he had been waiting for. After drawing three cards he gazed in delight at four queens and a seven of clubs in his hand. O'Connor must have thought he had a good hand too, for he went along when the judge covered the priest's £5 and raised him £5. When the priest responded by covering the £5 and raising £10, O'Connor lost his nerve and folded. Once again he was £12 down on where he had started playing.

The judge bit his thumbnail. Then he covered the priest's £10 and raised him £10.

'Five minutes to Tralee,' said the guard, poking his head round the compartment door. The priest stared in dismay at the matchsticks in the centre of the table and at his own small pile representing £12.

"I don't know,' he said. 'Oh, Lord, I don't know.'

'Father,' said O'Connor, 'you can't raise any more; you'll have to cover it and ask to see.'

'I suppose so,' said the priest sadly, pushing £10 in matchsticks into the centre of the table and leaving himself with £2. 'And I was doing so well. I should have given the orphanage the thirty-two pounds while I had it. And now I have only two pounds for them.'

'I'll make it up to five pounds, Father,' said Judge Comyn. 'There. Four ladies.'

O'Connor whistled. The priest looked at the spread-out queens and then at his own hand. 'Are not kings above queens?' he asked in puzzlement.

'They are if you have four of them,' said the judge.

The priest laid his cards on the table.

'But I do,' he said. And he did. 'Lord save us,' he breathed, 'but I thought all was lost. I thought you must have the royal thing there.'

They cleared the cards and matches away as they rolled into

Tralee. O'Connor got his cards back. The judge put the broken matches in the ashtray. O'Connor counted out twelve single pound notes from his pocket and handed them over to the priest.

'God bless you, my son,' said the priest.

Judge Comyn regretfully got out his cheque book. 'Fifty pounds exactly, I believe, Father,' he said.

'If you say so,' said the priest, 'sure and I have forgotten what we even started with.'

'I assure you I owe the orphanage fifty pounds,' said the judge. He prepared to write. 'You said the Dingle Orphanage? Is that what I should write?'

The priest appeared perplexed.

'You know, I do not believe they even have a bank account, so small is the place,' said the Father.

'Then I had better make it out to you personally,' said the judge, waiting for the name.

'But I do not have a bank account myself,' said the priest in bewilderment. 'I have never handled money.'

'There is a way round it,' said the judge urbanely. He wrote rapidly, tore out the cheque and offered it to the priest. 'This is made payable to bearer. The Bank of Ireland in Tralee will cash it and we are just in time. They close in thirty minutes.'

'You mean they will give me money at the bank for this?' asked the priest, holding the cheque carefully.

'Certainly,' said the judge, 'but be careful not to lose it. It is payable to the bearer, so anyone in possession of it would be able to cash it. Well now, O'Connor, Father, it has been a most interesting, albeit expensive trip. I must wish you good day.'

'And for me,' said O'Connor sadly. 'The Lord must have been dealing you the cards, Father. I've seldom seen such a hand. It'll be a lesson to me. No more playing cards on trains, least of all with the Church.'

'And I'll see the money is in the most deserving of orphanages before the sun sets,' said the priest.

They parted on Tralee station platform and Judge Comyn proceeded to his hotel. He wished for an early night before the start of the court hearings on the morrow.

The first two cases of the morning were very straightforward, being pleas of guilty for minor offences and he awarded fines in both cases. The empanelled jurors* of Tralee sat in enforced idleness.

Judge Comyn had his head bowed over his papers when the third defendant was called. Only the top of his judge's wig was visible to the court below.

'Put up Ronan Quirk O'Connor,' boomed the clerk to the court.

There was a scuffling of steps. The judge went on writing.

'You are Ronan Quirk O'Connor?' asked the clerk of the new defendant.

'I am,' said the voice.

'Ronan Quirk O'Connor,' said the clerk, 'you are charged with cheating at cards, contrary to Section 17 of the Gaming Act of 1845. In that you, Ronan Quirk O'Connor, on the 13th day of May of this year, in the County of Kerry, by fraud or unlawful device or ill-practice in playing at, or with, cards, won a sum of money from one Lurgan Keane to yourself. And thereby obtained the said sum of money from the said Lurgan Keane by false pretences. How say you to the charge? Guilty or not guilty?'

During this recitation Judge Comyn laid down his pen with unusual care, stared for a few more seconds at his papers as if wishing he could conduct the entire trial in this manner, and finally raised his eyes.

The wispy little man with the spaniel eyes stared back at him across the court in dumb amazement. Judge Comyn stared at the defendant in equal horror.

'Not guilty,' whispered O'Connor.

'One moment,' said the judge. The court sat in silence, staring at him as he sat impassive on his bench. Behind the mask of his face, his thoughts were in a turmoil. He could have stopped the case at once, claiming that he had an acquaintance with the defendant.

Then the thought occurred to him that this would have meant a retrial, since the defendant had now been formally charged, with all the extra costs to the taxpayer involved in that procedure. It came down, he told himself, to one question: could he trust himself to conduct the court fairly and well, and to give a true and fair summing up to the jury? He decided that he could.

'Swear in the jury, if you please,' he said.

This the clerk did, then inquired of O'Connor if he had legal representation. O'Connor said he did not, and wished to conduct his own defence. Judge Comyn swore to himself. Fairness would now demand that he bend over backwards to take the defendant's part against prosecuting counsel.

This gentleman now rose to present the facts which, he said, were simple enough. On 13 May last, a grocer from Tralee, one Lurgan Keane, had boarded the Dublin to Tralee train in Dublin to return home. He happened perchance to be carrying a quantity of cash upon his person, to wit, £71.

During the course of the journey he had entered into a game of chance with the defendant and another party, using a pack of cards produced by the defendant. So remarkable had been the losses he had incurred that he became suspicious. At Farranfore, one stop before Tralee, he had descended from the train on an excuse, approached a servant of the railway company and asked that the police at Tralee be present upon the platform.

His first witness was a police sergeant of the Tralee force, a large, solid man who gave evidence of arrest. He swore that, acting on information received, he had been present at Tralee station on 13 May last, when the Dublin train rolled in. There he had been approached by a man he later knew to be Mr Lurgan Keane, who had pointed out to him the defendant.

He had asked the defendant to accompany him to Tralee police station, which the man did. There he was required to turn out his pockets. Among the contents was a pack of cards which Mr Keane identified as those that had been used in a game of poker upon the train.

These, he said, had been sent to Dublin for examination and upon receipt of the report from Dublin the accused O'Connor had been charged with the offence.

So far, so clear. The next witness was from the Fraud Squad of the Garda in Dublin. He had evidently been on the train of yesterday, mused the judge, but travelling third class.

The detective constable swore that upon close examination the deck of cards had been seen to be a marked deck. The prosecuting counsel held up a deck of cards and the detective identified it by his own mark. The deck was passed to him. In what way were the cards marked, inquired counsel.

'In two manners, my lord,' the detective told the judge. 'By what is called "shading" and "trimming". Each of the four suits is indicated on the back of the cards by trimming the edges at different places, on each end of the card so that it does not matter which way up the card is held. In the trimming, the white border between the edge of the pattern and the edge of the card is caused to vary in width. This variation, though very slight, can be observed from across the table, thus indicating to the cheat what suits his opponent is holding. If that is clear?'

'A model of lucidity,' said Judge Comyn, staring at O'Connor.

'The high cards, from ace down to ten, were distinguished from each other by shading, that is, using a chemical preparation to cause slight darkening or lightening of tiny areas of the pattern on the backs of the cards. The areas so affected are extremely small, sometimes no larger than the tip of one whorl in the complex pattern. But enough to be spotted by the cardsharp* from across the table, because he knows exactly what he is looking for.'

'Would it be necessary for the cardsharp to deal dishonestly as well?' asked counsel. He was aware the jury was riveted. It made such a change from stealing horses.

'A crooked deal might be included,' conceded the detective from the Fraud Squad, 'but it would not be necessary.'

'Would it be possible to win against such a player?' asked counsel.

'Quite impossible, sir,' the witness told the bench. 'The cardsharp would simply decline to wager when he knew his opponent had a better hand, and place high bets when he knew his own was better.'

'No further questions,' said counsel. For the second time O'Connor declined to cross-examine.

'You have the right to ask the witness any question you may wish, concerning his evidence,' Judge Comyn told the accused.

'Thank you, my lord,' said O'Connor, but kept his peace.

Counsel's third, last and star witness was the Tralee grocer, Lurgan Keane, who entered the witness box as a bull to the arena and glared at O'Connor.

Prompted by the prosecuting counsel, he told his story. He had concluded a business deal in Dublin that day, which accounted for the large amount of cash he had been carrying. In the train, he had been inveigled into a game of poker, at which he thought he was a skilled player, and before Farranfore had been relieved of £62. He had become suspicious because, however promising the hand he held, he had always been bettered by another and had lost money.

At Farranfore he had descended from the train, convinced he had been cheated, and had asked for the police to be present at Tralee.

'And I was right,' he roared to the jury, 'your man was playing with marked cards.'

The twelve good men and true* nodded solemnly.

This time O'Connor rose, looking sadder than ever and as harmless as a calf in the byre, to cross-examine. Mr Keane glowered at him.

'You say that I produced the pack of cards?' he asked sorrowfully.

'You did,' said Keane.

'In what manner?' asked O'Connor.

Keane looked puzzled. 'From your pocket,' he said.

'Yes,' agreed O'Connor, 'from my pocket. But what did I do with the cards?'

Keane thought for a moment. 'You began to play patience,' he said.

Judge Comyn, who had almost begun to believe in the possibility of the law of remarkable coincidence, got that sinking feeling again.

'And did I speak first to you,' asked the accused, 'or did you speak first to me?'

The burly grocer looked crestfallen. 'I spoke to you,' he said, then turning to the jury he added, 'but your man was playing so badly I could not help it. There were blacks on reds and reds on blacks that he couldn't see, so I pointed a couple out to him.'

'But when it came to the poker,' persisted O'Connor, 'did I suggest a friendly game of poker or did you?'

'You did,' said Keane heatedly, 'and you suggested we make it interesting with a little wagering. Wagering indeed. Sixty-two pounds is a lot of money.'

The jury nodded again. It was indeed. Enough to keep a working man for almost a year.

'I put it to you,' said O'Connor to Keane, 'that it was *you* who suggested the poker, and *you* who proposed the wager. Before that we were playing with matchsticks?'

The grocer thought hard. The honesty shone from his face. Something stirred in his memory. He would not lie.

'It may have been me,' he conceded, then a new thought came to him. He turned to the jury. 'But isn't that the whole skill of it? Isn't that just what the cardsharp does? He *inveigles* his victim into a game.'

He was obviously in love with the word 'inveigle' which the judge thought was new to his vocabulary. The jurymen nodded. Quite obviously they too would hate to be inveigled.

'One last point,' said O'Connor sadly, 'when we settled up, how much did you pay me?'

'Sixty-two pounds,' said Keane angrily. 'Hard-earned money.'

'No,' said O'Connor from the dock, 'how much did you lose to *me*, personally?'

The grocer from Tralee thought hard. His face dropped. 'Not to you,' he said. 'Nothing. It was the farmer who won.'

'And did I win from him?' asked O'Connor, by now looking on the edge of tears.

'No,' said the witness. 'You lost about eight pounds.'

'No further questions,' said O'Connor.

Mr Keane was about to step down when the judge's voice recalled him. 'One moment, Mr Keane. You say "the farmer won"? Who exactly was this farmer?'

'The other man in the compartment, my lord. He was a farmer from Wexford. Not a good player, but he had the devil's own luck.'

'Did you manage to get his name?' asked Judge Comyn.

Mr Keane looked perplexed. 'I did not,' he said. 'It was the accused who had the cards. He was trying to cheat me all right.'

The prosecution case ended and O'Connor took the stand on his own behalf. He was sworn in. His story was as simple as it was plaintive. He bought and sold horses for a living; there was no crime in that. He enjoyed a friendly game of cards, but was no dab hand at it. A week before the train journey of 13 May he had been having a quiet stout in a Dublin public house when he felt a hard lump on the wooden pew near his thigh.

It was a pack of cards, apparently abandoned by a previous occupant of the booth, and certainly not new. He thought of handing them in to the barman, but realized such a time-worn pack would have no value anyway. He had kept them, and amused himself with patience on his long journeys seeking a foal or mare to buy for clients.

If the cards were marked, he was totally ignorant of it. He knew nothing of this shading and trimming the detective had talked about. He would not even know what to look for on the backs of his pack of cards, found on a pub seat.

As for cheating, didn't cheats win? he asked the jury. He had lost £8 10s. on that journey, to a complete stranger. He was a fool to himself, for the farmer had had all the run of the good hands. If Mr Keane had wagered and lost more than he, that was perhaps because Mr Keane was a more rash man than he. But as to cheating, he would have no part of it, and certainly he would not have lost so much of his own hard-earned money.

In cross-examination prosecuting counsel sought to break his story. But the wispy little man stuck to it with apologetic and self-deprecating tenacity. Finally counsel had to sit down.

O'Connor returned to the dock and awaited the summing up. Judge Comyn gazed at him across the court. You're a poor specimen, O'Connor, he thought. Either your story is true, in which case you are a truly unlucky card-player. Or it is not, in which case you must be the world's most incompetent card-sharp. Either way, you have twice lost, using your own cards, to strangers in railway trains.

On the matter of the summing-up, however, he could allow no such choice. He pointed out to the jury that the accused had claimed he had found the cards in a Dublin pub and was completely unaware that they were a marked deck. The jury might privately wish to believe that story or not; the fact was the prosecution had not disproved it, and in Irish law the burden of proof was upon them.

Secondly, the accused had claimed that it was not he but Mr Keane who had proposed both the poker and the wagering, and Mr Keane had conceded that this might be true.

But much more importantly, the prosecution case was that the accused had won money by false pretences from the witness Lurgan Keane. Whatever the pretences, true or false, witness Keane had conceded on oath that the accused had won no money from him. Both he, the witness, and the accused had lost money, albeit widely differing sums. On that issue the case must fail. It was his duty to direct the jury to acquit the defendant. Knowing his court, he also pointed out that it lacked fifteen minutes to the hour of luncheon.

It takes a case of weighty jurisprudence to keep a Kerry jury from its lunch, and the twelve good men were back in ten minutes with a verdict of not guilty. O'Connor was discharged and left the dock.

Judge Comyn disrobed behind the court in the robing room, hung his wig on a peg and left the building to seek his own lunch. Without robes, ruffle* or wig, he passed through the throng on the pavement before the court house quite unrecognized.

He was about to cross the road to the town's principal hotel where, he knew, a fine Shannon salmon awaited his attention, when he saw coming out of the hotel yard a handsome and gleaming limousine of noted marque*. At the wheel was O'Connor.

'Do you see your man?' asked a wondering voice by his side. He glanced to his right and found the Tralee grocer standing beside him.

'I do,' he said.

The limousine swept out of the hotel yard. Sitting beside O'Connor was a passenger dressed all in black.

'Do you see who's sitting beside him?' asked Keane in wonderment.

The car swished towards them. The cleric with a concern to help the orphans of Dingle bestowed a benign smile and raised two stiff fingers towards the men on the sidewalk. Then the car was heading down the street.

'Was that an ecclesiastical blessing?' asked the grocer.

'It might have been,' conceded Judge Comyn, 'though I doubt it.'

'And what was he dressed in those clothes for?' asked Lurgan Keane.

'Because he's a priest of the Holy Church,' said the judge.

'He never is,' said the grocer hotly, 'he's a farmer from Wexford.'

NOTES

whiskery thornproof (p78)
   a strong, heavy woollen material
weskit (p78)
   (alternative spelling of) waistcoat
Eamon de Valera (p79)
   Irish statesman and Prime Minister (1882–1975)
Dail (p79)
   the lower house of the Irish Parliament
Cardinal Newman (p81)
   a noted Catholic theologian (1801–90)
Havana (p83)
   a good quality cigar (from Havana in Cuba)
fold (your hand) (p83)
   stop playing
ace high (p84)
   a hand of mixed cards containing one ace
like the confessional (p85)
   kept secret (like words spoken to a priest in the confessional box)
wain (p86)
   (Irish) child
the empanelled jurors (p91)
   people who have been enrolled (empanelled) as members of a jury
cardsharp (p94)
   a person who cheats others at cards
the twelve good men and true (p95)
   a literary phrase for the twelve members of the jury
ruffle (p98)
   a frill worn at the neck – part of the judge's formal costume
of noted marque (p99)
   of a well-known, fashionable brand

DISCUSSION

1 What kind of person is Judge Comyn? Are there aspects of his
   character that make him an easy target for a deception of this kind?
   Does your view of him change in the second part of the story (after the
   train ride ends)?

2 How do you think Judge Comyn feels at the end of the story – angry, resigned, amused? How much was he himself to blame, do you think, for being tricked?

3 Describe the way the two tricksters set up the deception. Was it cleverly done, in your opinion? Should the judge have suspected something?

4 Do the two card players deserve congratulation or punishment? If they have done wrong, do you consider them to be serious criminals or simply rogues? What might be a suitable punishment?

LANGUAGE FOCUS

1 Find these expressions in the text and explain them in simple English.

- *'It was a sight too close for comfort . . .'* (p79)
- *'You have the knack of the cards.'* (p82)
- *''Tis the very thing.'* (p83)
- *'In for a penny, in for a pound.'* (p87)
- *Fairness would now demand that he bend over backwards to take the defendant's part against prosecuting counsel.* (p92)
- *Judge Comyn . . . got that sinking feeling again.* (p95)
- *He was a fool to himself, for the farmer had had all the run of the good hands.* (p97)

2 What do these sentences reveal to us about the judge?

- *. . . he did not wish to start a conversation, having been schooled in England.* (p79)
- *The editor was a man who had his priorities right, thought Judge Comyn.* (p79)
- *Judge Comyn laid down his pen with unusual care . . .* (p91)

ACTIVITIES

1 Suppose that O'Connor and his accomplice decide to pass on to a friend their method of tricking money out of people. Write a set of instructions (not including details of the actual poker game) about suitable places, timing, disguises, supporting stories, victims, and so on.

2 As O'Connor and the priest (or farmer) sweep past the judge and Mr Keane in their grand limousine after the trial, they must have plenty to talk about. Write down a short conversation for them.

EDNA, BACK FROM AMERICA

THE AUTHOR

Clare Boylan was born in Dublin in 1948. She worked as a journalist for ten years before beginning to write fiction. Her first novel, *Holy Pictures*, was a huge success, and was translated into several languages. Subsequent novels include *Last Resorts, Home Rule, Black Baby*, and *Beloved Stranger*. She has also produced three short story collections, *A Nail on the Head, Concerning Virgins*, and *That Bad Woman*. Her short stories have appeared in many anthologies, and one of them, 'Some Ladies on a Tour', was the basis for the film *Making Waves*, which was nominated for an Oscar in 1988. Her work casts a wry and sympathetic look at life in Ireland today, and shows particular insight into the lives of Catholic women.

THE STORY

When you're tired of yourself, of your way of life, of everything, what do you do? Some re-invent themselves; some sigh and carry on; some, the truly desperate, put an end to everything. But what if you could become somebody else – if you could walk into another person's life and adopt their clothes, their habits, their relationships?

June, miserable, desperate, and about to kill herself, is suddenly given the opportunity to do just this. She is offered a new identity and a new existence. This is her chance for a fresh start, a better and happier life. It seems almost too good to be true . . .

EDNA, BACK FROM AMERICA

She went up to the water's edge and peered in. 'Go on,' she urged herself. 'Can't be much worse than a cold shower.' She lit a cigarette to feel something glowing other than the cabaret sign on the hotel behind her.

She remembered this place when she was ten years of age – a row of boarding houses in different colours fanned out along the prom like biscuits on a plate. When she had got off the train with her dad she'd thought that this was where it stopped at the end of the world. A donkey in a hat waited patiently to take them to the bottom of the beach. And then back. There wasn't anywhere else to go at the end of the world. All week they ate chips and went for donkey-rides and made pies out of the sand. He left her on her own at night but she didn't complain. She wanted to seem *soigné**. *Soigné* was a word he used. She couldn't believe it when the week came to an end. She saw the look of pity on his face, the rueful way his lips soothed the stem of his pipe. She was doing what he called a war dance. He took her back to Mum and Mr Boothroyd.

It was all changed now, cabaret hotels and karaoke lounges and hamburger palaces. Everything's different except me, she thought. I haven't changed since I was ten. Nobody wanted me then and nobody cares about me now. She sighed and threw away her cigarette. She began to scale the blue and gold railing. Behind her a crowd started to cheer.

She could hear car doors banging and a lot of excited noise as the cabaret hotel disgorged its patrons. 'Hell,' said June and she stepped down from the railing.

'Edna!' a woman kept calling out.

What would she do now? She hadn't the price of a hotel room.

'It is! It's Edna! Back from America!'

She turned around to discourage whoever was making the noise. A woman in a fur coat ran right up to her and plucked at her leather jacket with little fidgeting hands. 'Edna!' she cried, her eyes glittering with greed as if she was calling 'housey housey*'.

'I'm not Edna,' June backed away.

The woman frowned. 'Don't you know me? Muriel!' She put out a hand and took it back again. 'Where's your things?'

'I've got nothing.'

'Your handbag?'

Sullenly June showed her hands in which only a pack of cigarettes was held. She shoved them back in her pockets.

The woman nodded. 'You've come as you went.' She seemed quite pleased. 'Everyone took it as proof when you left your handbag behind. No woman leaves without a handbag, they said. Not unless she's dead. You don't know Edna, I told them.'

'I'm not Edna,' June said. 'You've made a mistake.'

'No I haven't.' She wouldn't accept anything.

'Now look here . . .!' June began angrily, but her mind had gone blank. She stared wearily past the woman out to sea. Rain had started and the tide lapped delicately at the little mousey shards. Hell, it looked cold. If she had gone into the water and been fished out the following day there would be nothing to identify her. The woman called Muriel would turn up and swear that she was Edna. She began to laugh. Muriel watched her warily and then she too started to titter. 'You've not lost your sense of humour, Edna. You always were a tease. Now let's not stand here getting soaked to the skin when we could be home by the fire with a nice drop of scotch. You still like scotch, don't you?'

Here was one argument that June need not resist. 'Yes.'

♧

They were settled around the Tudor-style fireplace with glasses of scotch in Muriel's mock-period house when Ted appeared.

'Ted! Look who's here!' Muriel challenged. A big man, uneasy in his successful suit, studied June seriously but without much hope, as if she was an examination paper.

'It's Edna!'

'Back from America!' the woman prompted.

'Edna!' He blew air through his teeth. 'America?' He studied her closely while he refuelled her glass. At last he nodded. 'You'd best stay here until things are sorted out.'

As she fell asleep in a room where everything was in matched shades of lavender, she wondered about Edna, what trick of personality she had to make herself so welcome to Ted and his wife while she, apparently with the same face, had no one. Maybe she and Edna were related. Funny how her dad had picked out this place. Perhaps he had a girlfriend there once and left her pregnant. Men were such bastards. Even Alastair. She'd accepted him without question, she'd loved him and nursed him through his illness. When he died there was only the house and its memories. Then his wife turned up. She never knew he'd been married. Alastair's small wealth had gone to her – a woman he had not seen in fifteen years. She was left with nothing. On the train on her way to this place where she had once been happy, a friendly youth talked to her and after he got off at his station she realised that he had taken her handbag. She was relieved in a way, for there was now no smallest point in carrying on another day.

'You've gone arty,' Muriel observed over breakfast.

Quickly June said that she hadn't gone anything, that she still wore the same style she had adopted in her student days. She had meant to leave early in the morning, to complete her mission at dawn on the deserted pier. Absurdly, she had slept it out. 'Look, I'm not your friend. You've been very kind, but I don't know you.'

The woman looked crestfallen. Then she began to cry. 'I'd

know you anywhere.'

'I had nowhere to go,' June apologised. 'I hadn't any money.'

'Is that all?' The childish face dried in an instant. 'You always were too proud.' Muriel sat down heavily. 'Look love, I've got bad news and good. Your mum's passed on. I'm sorry. It's four years ago now. She left a bit of money for you.'

'How much?' June said.

'She didn't have much. Five thousand pounds. And of course there's her cottage.'

Later on, Muriel drove her to see the cottage, to show how she had tended the garden. It was a safe, and modest little house, guarded by lupins and red hot pokers*. June, who was homeless, had an urge to move in right away. It was like a fairy story. She knew she must make the truth known to Muriel but she could not bear to break the spell.

It was Muriel's suggestion that she should revert to her old hairstyle. She allowed herself to be led to a dangerously homely looking establishment where a big woman called Beattie greeted her with wonder before holding her down like a sheep to be sheared. As she gripped and snipped, Beattie talked about the old days. The lives of women had not changed here as they had everywhere else. It was like a dance in which one changed partners for a brief number of years and when the music stopped, when you reached twenty-four or five, you stayed for the rest of your life with whatever partner happened to be opposite you. Terry had ended up with Renee, Joe and Sarah had a child who was backward, Bill Ferret, who used to look like Elvis, had gone bald and Sid and Sylvie weren't getting on too well.

'Sid and Sylvie,' June echoed distantly, thinking how well their names got on.

'Beattie,' Muriel warned.

They grew silent, watching each other in the mirror as Edna's face was summoned up under the scissors. Had Edna been abandoned by Sid in favour of Sylvie? Was that why she went all the way to America? Perhaps June and Edna had something in common after all. Beattie had cut her hair into a mound of uneven bangs that gave her an odd, rakish appearance. What would Alastair make of her now? She realised it didn't matter any more.

'There!' Beattie said at last. 'There's your old self for you. All you need now is your old accent. Fat lot of good that'll do you.'

As Muriel introduced her to Edna's old haunts, June discovered that the village hadn't really changed at all. It was the visitors to the pier that had altered, demanding an up-date of the town's single attraction – the donkey.

Alice Cranmer's fashion shop still had slips and lemon twinsets in the windows. Girls tried on pink lipstick in the chemist shop. A small dairy displayed faded windmills and postcards and sold damp ice-cream cones. June liked it. She knew that she must someday leave but for the moment she hung about Muriel watching for clues. 'You won't mind my saying, but I preferred your old style,' Muriel offered. Meekly she submitted to Mrs Harkins who pinned her into an assortment of close-fitting Doris Day* dresses and costumes. She had her hair lightened and learned to walk on high-heeled sling-backs. When Muriel ceremoniously handed over Edna's old handbag, with its letters and photographs and shopping lists, June did not receive it as a final clue to the other woman's past, but as the lifting of a cloud of amnesia. Everyone accepted her. The one or two who had glanced at her suspiciously soon embraced her and she thought it was not because they had overcome their doubts but because they needed Edna. She was puzzled by the woman who had fled this simple, rich life. She felt entitled to take what Edna had thrown away.

It was a shock to discover that Edna had thrown away a husband and daughter.

She found the snapshot in Edna's handbag, a thin man with a solemn girl of eight or nine. 'Sid and Sylvie, Clipton Pier, 1983,' she read out from the pencilled caption on the back.

'You wouldn't recognise your little girl now,' Muriel shook her head. 'Sid hasn't changed much. Your husband never changes.'

June's attention was on the little girl, a child like herself who could not hold love. Edna had walked out on her own daughter. The thought of it brought tears to June's eyes.

'Maybe it's time you went home, love,' Muriel said gently. Ted and me don't want to rush you, but everyone's been notified. They're only waiting for you.'

On the way to the cottage she counted up the signs by which Sid might recognise her as an imposter. Had Edna a scar or mole? Was she eager or reluctant in bed. 'I'll make it work,' she determined. 'A month ago I had no one. Now I've got friends, a family, and a home. I'll make them want me even if they find out I'm not Edna.' She felt calm. It was Muriel who was nervous. 'About Sylvie,' she said at last. 'I should have told you. She's no better.'

'I'll take care of her,' June said quickly. She was used to sick people. She had taken care of Alastair.

Muriel sighed. 'They won't keep her in anywhere. Not even that mental place.

'Remember the time she set fire to the rabbit? She did it to a boy in the last home.'

June lit a cigarette. She drew on it as if draining a pond with a straw. 'Why couldn't Sid take care of Sylvie?'

Muriel looked uncomfortable. 'He's been inside again. Got in a fight with a man and left him in a very bad way. It's the drink, Edna. You know that. But he's promised he'll never lay a hand on *you* again. There was some around here that thought he'd done away with you. I never believed that. Well, I have to believe the best of my own brother. Anyway Sid'll behave with mother around. She's still a battle-axe, even though she's daft as a brush.'

'His mother?' June raked at her face and hair with her fingers as if a growth of cobwebs enclosed her.

'They threw her out of that Haven place* now she's wetting*. It's Alzheimer's*.'

'Sid's your brother?' June disciplined her panic with reason. 'Then we're talking about your mother too. Why can't you take her?'

'I'm sorry, love. Ted won't have it. I didn't admit I was at my wits' end until you turned up.'

'Stop the car, Muriel,' June said. 'I'm not Edna.'

Muriel tittered excitedly. 'You've left that a bit late. They're all waiting for you back at the cottage!'

She tried the door, which was secured by a central locking device. 'Please let me out. I'm not Edna. My name's June Pritchard.'

The other woman took her eye off the road to sharply assess her passenger. 'You won't mind my saying, but that pearly shadow makes your eyes pop.' She returned her attention to the road and her plump foot squeezed the accelerator. 'You should draw your eye-liner out at the edges, like you used to.'

NOTES

soigné (p103)
    elegant and well-groomed
housey housey (p104)
    another name for bingo, a popular gambling game; the winner calls
    'housey housey' to claim their prize
red hot poker (p106)
    a garden plant with a tall, brightly coloured flower spike
Doris Day (p107)
    a singer and film star popular in the 1950s and 60s as the pretty,
    innocent star of romantic comedies
that Haven place (p109)
    a home for the elderly who are too frail or sick to live alone
wetting (p109)
    making her bed or clothes wet through accidentally urinating
Alzheimer's (p109)
    a disease affecting especially older people, which causes loss of
    memory, speech, movement, and the ability to think clearly

DISCUSSION

1 What do you think motivates Muriel to identify June as Edna? Does
   she act on the spur of the moment when she sees June at the water's
   edge, or has she been searching for some time for someone who can
   solve her problems for her? Do you think she really believes that June is
   Edna?

2 June has always been the victim of other people's deceptions. What
   instances of this in the past are mentioned in the story?

3 What do you think motivates June to accept the role of Edna? Is it
   greed? loneliness? the wish to belong somewhere? the idea of getting
   something for nothing? What things does Muriel offer that persuade
   June to play the game? Or does June simply accept passively the new
   role that life has handed to her?

4 How did you feel about the ending of the story? Was this a satisfactory
   point at which to end, or would you have preferred the story to
   continue, telling us whether Edna accepted the circumstances, now
   revealed in all their horror, or ran away from them?

Language Focus

1 *He took her back to Mum and Mr Boothroyd.* (p103)
   Who is Mr Boothroyd?

2 *What would she do now? She hadn't the price of a hotel room.* (p103)
   What is the point of mentioning the hotel room?

3 *'Edna!' she cried, her eyes glittering with greed . . .* (p104)
   Why with greed?

4 *She was relieved in a way, for there was now no smallest point in carrying on another day.* (p105)
   What does this reveal to us about June's personality?

5 *They grew silent, watching each other in the mirror as Edna's face was summoned up under the scissors.* (p107)
   June is not just having a haircut. What process is taking place here?

6 *June lit a cigarette. She drew on it as if draining a pond with a straw.* (p108)
   What is the writer trying to convey here?

7 *June raked at her face and hair with her fingers as if a growth of cobwebs enclosed her.* (p109)
   What is, in fact, enclosing June at this point? Why is a 'cobweb' a good metaphor to use here?

Activities

1 What do you suppose did happen to Edna? Did she run away from an intolerable situation? Did she kill herself? Did Sid kill her? Write a paragraph explaining what you think and why.

2 What do you think Muriel's thoughts are on the final day of the story? What happens when she delivers Edna to her husband, daughter, and mother-in-law? Write an entry for Muriel's diary outlining the events of the day and how she feels about them.

3 What happens next? Does June run away? Does she decide to try and live with the situation? Write a conclusion for the story.

4 Do you think *Edna, Back from America* is a good title? Why, or why not? What other titles can you think of that would suit the story?

NEIGHBOURS

THE AUTHOR

Paul Theroux was born in Medford, Massachusetts in 1941. He studied at the University of Massachusetts, and his first novel *Waldo* was published in 1967. He then spent five years in Africa and three in Singapore, lecturing and writing. While in Africa he became friends with V. S. Naipaul (author of *The Coward* in this volume), but their thirty-year friendship ended bitterly on the publication of Theroux's book *Sir Vidia's Shadow* in 1998, in which he was deeply critical of Naipaul's character and his hasty second marriage. Among his best-known novels are *Saint Jack* (1973) and *The Mosquito Coast* (1981), both of which have been filmed, and he has also achieved fame with his travel books. Theroux often considers life from the viewpoint of an expatriate: interested in the foreign life surrounding him, but in a rather detached, dispassionate way. He now lives in England and America.

THE STORY

Keeping up good relations with your neighbours can be delicate and difficult, particularly when people live close together in the same building, share the same staircase, and can hear the noise their neighbours make – sometimes, it seems, deliberately and thoughtlessly.

The American diplomat in this story has two neighbours in his London apartment block. One of them, Wigley, is a quiet and unobtrusive man who works for the Post Office, and who seems friendly in an undemanding way. Maybe they can join forces against the noisy, obnoxious Corner Door, who keeps late hours, and whose huge motorbike blocks up the entrance way . . .

Neighbours

I had two neighbours at Overstrand Mansions – we shared the same landing, In America 'neighbour' has a friendly connotation; in England it is a chilly word, nearly always a stranger, a map reference more than anything else. One of my neighbours was called R. Wigley; the other had no nameplate.

It did not surprise me at all that Corner Door had no nameplate. He owned a motorcycle and kept late nights. He wore leather – I heard it squeak; and boots – they hit the stairs like hammers on an anvil. His motorcycle was a Kawasaki – Japanese of course, the British are only patriotic in the abstract, and they can be traitorously frugal – tax-havens are full of Brits. They want value for money, even when they are grease-monkeys*, bikers with skinny faces and sideburns and teeth missing, wearing jackboots and swastikas. That was how I imagined Corner Door, the man in 4C.

I had never seen his face, though I had heard him often enough. His hours were odd, he was always rushing off at night and returning in the early morning – waking me when he left and waking me again when he came back. He was selfish and unfriendly, scatterbrained, thoughtless – no conversation but plenty of bike noise. I pictured him wearing one of those German helmets that looks like a kettle, and I took him to be a coward at heart, who sneaked around whining until he had his leather suit and his boots on, until he mounted his too-big Japanese motorcycle, which he kept in the entryway of Overstrand Mansions, practically blocking it. When he was suited up and mounted on his bike he was a Storm Trooper with blood in his eye.

It also struck me that this awful man might be a woman, an awful woman. But even after several months there I never saw the person from 4C face to face. I saw him – or her – riding away, his back, the chrome studs patterned on his jacket. But women didn't behave like this. It was a man.

R. Wigley was quite different – he was a civil servant, Post Office, Welsh I think, very methodical. He wrote leaflets. The Post Office issued all sorts of leaflets – explaining pensions, television licences, road-tax, driving permits, their savings bank and everything else, including of course stamps. The leaflets were full of directions and advice. In this complicated literate country you were expected to read your way out of difficulty.

When I told Wigley I wouldn't be in London much longer than a couple of years he became hospitable. No risk, you see. If I had been staying for a long time he wouldn't have been friendly – wouldn't have dared. Neighbours are a worry, they stare, they presume, they borrow things, they ask you to forgive them their trespasses*. In the most privacy-conscious country in the world neighbours are a problem. But I was leaving in a year or so, and I was an American diplomat – maybe I was a spy! He suggested I call him Reg.

We met at the Prince Albert* for a drink. A month later, I had him over with the Scadutos, Vic and Marietta, and it was then that talk turned to our neighbours. Wigley said there was an actor on the ground floor and that several country Members of Parliament lived in Overstrand Mansions when the Commons was sitting*. Scaduto asked him blunt questions I would not have dared to ask, but I was glad to hear his answers. Rent? Thirty-seven pounds a week. Married? Had been – no longer. University? Bristol. And, when he asked Wigley about his job, Scaduto listened with fascination and then said, 'It's funny, but I never actually imagined anyone writing those things. It doesn't seem like real writing.'

Good old Skiddoo*.

Wigley said, 'I assure you, it's quite real.'

Scaduto went on interrogating him – Americans were tremendous questioners – but noticing Wigley's discomfort made me reticent. The British confined conversation to neutral impersonal subjects, resisting any effort to be trapped into friendship. They got to know each other by allowing details to slip out, little mentions which, gathered together, became revelations. The British liked having secrets – they had lost so much else – and that was one of their secrets.

Scaduto asked, 'What are your other neighbours like?'

I looked at Wigley. I wondered what he would say. I would not have dared to put the question to him.

He said, 'Some of them are incredibly noisy and others downright frightening.'

This encouraged me. I said, 'Our Nazi friend with the motorcycle, for one.'

Had I gone too far?

'I was thinking of that prig, Hurst,' Wigley said, 'who has the senile Labrador that drools and squitters* all over the stairs.'

'I've never seen our motorcyclist,' I said. 'But I've heard him. The bike. The squeaky leather shoulders. The boots.' I caught Wigley's eye. 'It's just the three of us on this floor, I guess.'

I had lived there just over two months without seeing anyone else.

Wigley looked uncertain, but said, 'I suppose so.'

'My kids would love to have a motorcycle,' Marietta Scaduto said. 'I've got three hulking boys, Mr Wigley.'

I said, 'Don't let them bully you into buying one.'

'Don't you worry,' Marietta said. 'I think those things are a menace.'

'Some of them aren't so bad,' Wigley said. 'Very economical.' He glanced at me. 'So I've heard.'

'It's kind of an image-thing, really. Your psychologists will tell you all about it.' Skiddoo was pleased with himself: he liked analysing human behaviour – 'deviants' were his favourites, he said. 'It's classic textbook-case stuff. The simp* plays big tough guy on his motorcycle. Walter Mitty* turns into Marlon Brando*. It's an aggression thing. Castration complex. What do you do for laughs, Reg?'

Wigley said, 'I'm not certain what you mean by laughs.'

'Fun,' Scaduto said. 'For example, we've got one of these home computers. About six thousand bucks, including some accessories – hardware, software. Christ, we've had hours of fun with it. The kids love it.'

'I used to be pretty keen on aircraft,' Wigley said, and looked very embarrassed saying so, as if he were revealing an aberration in his boyhood.

Scaduto said, 'Keen in what way?'

'Taking snaps of them,' Wigley said.

'Snaps?' Marietta Scaduto said. She was smiling.

'Yes,' Wigley said. 'I had one of those huge Japanese cameras that can do anything. They're absolutely idiot-proof and fiendishly expensive.'

'I never thought anyone taking dinky little pictures of planes could be described as "keen".' Scaduto said the word like a brand-name for ladies' underwear.

'Some of them were big pictures,' Wigley said coldly.

'Even big pictures,' Scaduto said. 'I could understand flying in the planes, though. Getting inside, and air-borne, and doing the loop-the-loop.'

Wigley said, 'They were bombers.'

'Now you're talking, Reg!' Scaduto's sudden enthusiasm warmed the atmosphere a bit, and they continued to talk about aeroplanes.

'My father had an encyclopaedia,' Wigley said. 'You looked up "aeroplane". It said, "Aeroplane: See Flying-Machine." '

Later, Marietta said, 'These guys on their motorcycles, I was just thinking. They really have a problem. Women never do stupid things like that.'

Vic Scaduto said, 'Women put on long gowns, high heels, padded bras. They pile their hair up, they pretend they're princesses. That's worse, fantasy-wise. Or they get into really tight provocative clothes, all tits and ass, swinging and bouncing, lipstick, the whole bit, cleavage hanging down. And then – I'm not exaggerating – and then they say, "Don't touch me or I'll scream." '

Good old Skiddoo.

'You've got a big problem if you think that,' Marietta said. She spoke then to Wigley. 'Sometimes the things he says are sick.'

Wigley smiled and said nothing.

'And he works for the government,' Marietta said. 'You wouldn't think so, would you?'

That was it. The Scadutos went out arguing, and Wigley left: a highly successful evening, I thought.

Thanks to Scaduto's pesterings I knew much more about Wigley. He was decent, he was reticent, and I respected him for the way he handled Good Old Skiddoo. And we were no more friendly than before – that was all right with me: I didn't want to be burdened with his friendship any more than he wanted to be lumbered with mine. I only wished that the third tenant on our floor was as gracious a neighbour as Wigley.

Would Wigley join me in making a complaint? He said he'd rather not. That was the British way – don't make a fuss, Reg.

He said, 'To be perfectly frank, he doesn't actually bother me.'

This was the first indication I'd had that it was definitely a man, not a woman.

'He drives me up the wall sometimes. He keeps the craziest hours. I've never laid eyes on him, but I know he's weird.'

Wigley smiled at me and I immediately regretted saying, 'He's weird,' because, saying so, I had revealed something of myself.

I said, 'I can't make a complaint unless you back me up.'

'I know.'

I could tell he thought I was being unfair. It created a little distance, this annoyance of mine that looked to him like intolerance. I knew this because Wigley had a girlfriend and didn't introduce me. A dozen times I heard them on the stairs. People who live alone are authorities on noises. I knew their laughs. I got to recognize the music, the bedsprings, the bathwater. He did not invite me over.

And of course there was my other subject, the Storm Trooper from 4C with his thumping jackboots at the oddest hours. I decided at last that wimpy little Wigley (as I now thought of him) had become friendly with him, perhaps ratted on me and told him that I disliked him.

Wigley worked at Post Office Headquarters, at St Martin's-le-Grand, taking the train to Victoria and then the tube to St Paul's. I sometimes saw him entering or leaving Battersea Park Station while I was at the bus stop. Occasionally, we walked together to or from Overstrand Mansions, speaking of the weather.

One day, he said, 'I might be moving soon.'

I felt certain he was getting married. I did not ask.

'Are you sick of Overstrand Mansions?'

'I need a bigger place.'

He was definitely getting married.

I had the large balcony apartment in front. Wigley had a two-room apartment just behind me. The motorcyclist's place I had never seen.

'I wish it were the Storm Trooper who was leaving, and not you.'

He was familiar with my name for the motorcyclist.

'Oh, well,' he said, and walked away.

Might be moving, he had said. It sounded pretty vague. But the following Friday he was gone. I heard noise and saw the moving van in front on Prince of Wales Drive. Bumps and curses echoed on the stairs. I didn't stir – too embarrassing to put him on the spot, especially as I had knocked on his door that morning hoping for the last time to get him to join me in a protest against the Storm Trooper. I'm sure he saw me through his spy-hole in the door – Wigley, I mean. But he didn't open. So he didn't care about the awful racket the previous night – boots, bangs, several screams. Wigley was bailing out and leaving me to deal with it.

He went without a word. Then I realized he had sneaked away. He had not said good-bye, I had never met his girlfriend, he was getting married – maybe already married. British neighbours!

I wasn't angry with him, but I was furious with the Storm Trooper who had created a misunderstanding between Wigley and me. Wigley had tolerated the noise and I had hated it and said so. The Storm Trooper had made me seem like a brute!

But I no longer needed Wigley's signature on a complaint. Now there were only two of us here. I could go in and tell him exactly what I thought of him. I could play the obnoxious American. Wigley's going gave me unexpected courage. I banged on his door and shook it, hoping that I was waking him up. There was no answer that day or any day. And there was no more noise, no Storm Trooper, no motorcycle, from the day Wigley left.

NOTES

grease monkey (p113)
(dated slang) a person who works with engines
forgive them their trespasses (p114)
forgive them for the things they do wrong (a reference to a line in the Christian prayer known as the Lord's Prayer)
the Prince Albert (p114)
a pub, named after the husband of Queen Victoria (1819–1901)
the Commons was sitting (p114)
the House of Commons (the elected British Parliament) was at work
Skiddoo (p114)
(US slang) go away; here, used as a nickname for Scaduto
squitter (p115)
(slang) to defecate
simp (p116)
(old-fashioned US slang) a simple or foolish person
Walter Mitty ... Marlon Brando (p116)
Walter Mitty, a quiet, mild little man who has fantasies of being heroic and successful, is a character in a short story by American writer James Thurber. The American film actor Marlon Brando first achieved fame as the rough, working-class hero of *A Streetcar Named Desire*.

DISCUSSION

1 At what point in the story did you begin to guess the identity of the Storm Trooper in 4C? What were the various pieces of evidence, and why do you think the narrator fails to draw the right conclusions?

2 Describe the narrator's attitude towards the British. Does it seem an appropriate one for a diplomat? How might it affect his judgement?

3 What role do the Scadutos play in the story? What do they tell us about the narrator, and about Wigley?

4 We are only given the narrator's viewpoint. How might Wigley view the narrator – as a threat, an interfering busybody, someone to be laughed at? Why do you think he allows the deception to continue?

5 The night before Wigley leaves there is an 'awful racket – boots, bangs, several screams'. What do you think is the reason for this? Revenge? Enjoyment? An attempt to provoke the narrator into a confrontation?

LANGUAGE FOCUS

1 Sometimes the narrator's thoughts are expressed in a very elliptical way. Try to explain the thinking behind these remarks.

> *No risk, you see.* (p114)
> *Good old Skiddoo.* (p114 and p117)
> *British neighbours!* (p119)

2 *It did not surprise me at all that Corner Door had no nameplate.* (p113)
Why not?

3 *In this complicated literate country you were expected to read your way out of difficulty.* (p114)
What does this indicate about the narrator's attitude? What other comments of his reveal the same attitude?

4 *'It's just the three of us on this floor, I guess.'* To this, Wigley replies, *'I suppose so.'* Is that an appropriate response? Is there anything strange about it? Later, Wigley mentions how economical motorcycles are, then adds, *'So I've heard'*. What is the significance of this addition, do you think?

5 *I immediately regretted saying, 'He's weird,' because, saying so, I had revealed something of myself.* (p118)
What is it that the narrator has revealed?

ACTIVITIES

1 *'A highly successful evening'* says the narrator when his guests leave. How might his guests describe it? Write a diary entry for Vic, Marietta, or Wigley, giving their view of the evening and the other guests.

2 Suppose that before Wigley leaves he writes a note saying goodbye to the narrator. What would he say? Would he reveal the truth about the motorcyclist, or would he prefer to leave the narrator to find out for himself? What would he say about the noise of the final night? Write the note that you think is most consistent with the character of Wigley.

3 Do you think 'Neighbours' is a good title for this story? If so, why? Would alternative titles, for example, 'The Storm Trooper' or 'Wigley's Secret', be more suitable or more interesting? Explain your reasons.

THE MODEL
MILLIONAIRE

THE AUTHOR

Oscar Wilde was born in Dublin in 1854 and studied at
Trinity College, Dublin, and at Oxford. He quickly
established himself as a prominent member of social and
literary circles in London, and began to make a name for
himself with his writings. These included poems and a
novel (*The Picture of Dorian Gray*), but he was most
celebrated for his witty, brilliant plays, such as *Lady
Windermere's Fan, The Importance of Being Earnest*, and
An Ideal Husband. He also wrote a number of shorter
works, including short stories and some classic children's
stories, which he wrote for his two sons. Wilde's
homosexuality brought him into conflict with the morals
of his time and he was sentenced to two years in prison,
after which he went to live in exile in Paris, where he died in
1900.

THE STORY

Most people would agree that you cannot count on good
looks and a charming personality to provide you with an
income in life. You also need to follow some kind of
occupation or profession and develop a talent for making
money.

Hughie Erskine discovers this truth to his cost. He is
handsome, charming, very popular, but he fails in every
job he tries and has very little money. Now he has fallen
deeply in love with a beautiful girl, but her father will not
agree to the marriage until Hughie has ten thousand
pounds. How can he possibly get such a sum? Then Hughie
meets somebody who seems to be in an even worse
financial situation than he is . . .

THE MODEL MILLIONAIRE

A note of admiration

Unless one is wealthy there is no use in being a charming fellow. Romance is the privilege of the rich, not the profession of the unemployed. The poor should be practical and prosaic. It is better to have a permanent income than to be fascinating. These are the great truths of modern life which Hughie Erskine never realised. Poor Hughie! Intellectually, we must admit, he was not of much importance. He never said a brilliant or even an ill-natured thing in his life. But then he was wonderfully good-looking, with his crisp brown hair, his clear-cut profile, and his grey eyes. He was as popular with men as he was with women, and he had every accomplishment except that of making money. His father had bequeathed him his cavalry sword, and a *History of the Peninsular War* in fifteen volumes. Hughie hung the first over his looking-glass, put the second on a shelf between Ruff's *Guide* and Bailey's *Magazine**, and lived on two hundred a year that an old aunt allowed him. He had tried everything. He had gone on the Stock Exchange for six months; but what was a butterfly to do among bulls and bears? He had been a tea-merchant for a little longer, but had soon tired of pekoe and souchong*. Then he had tried selling dry sherry. That did not answer; the sherry was a little too dry. Ultimately he became nothing, a delightful, ineffectual young man with a perfect profile and no profession.

To make matters worse, he was in love. The girl he loved was Laura Merton, the daughter of a retired Colonel who had lost his temper and his digestion in India, and had never found either of them again. Laura adored him, and he was ready to kiss her shoe-strings. They were the handsomest couple in London, and had not a penny-piece between them. The Colonel was very fond of

Hughie, but would not hear of any engagement.

'Come to me, my boy, when you have got ten thousand pounds of your own, and we will see about it,' he used to say; and Hughie looked very glum on those days, and had to go to Laura for consolation.

One morning, as he was on his way to Holland Park, where the Mertons lived, he dropped in to see a great friend of his, Alan Trevor. Trevor was a painter. Indeed, few people escape that nowadays. But he was also an artist, and artists are rather rare. Personally he was a strange rough fellow, with a freckled face and a red ragged beard. However, when he took up the brush he was a real master, and his pictures were eagerly sought after. He had been very much attracted by Hughie at first, it must be acknowledged, entirely on account of his personal charm. 'The only people a painter should know,' he used to say, 'are people who are *bête** and beautiful, people who are an artistic pleasure to look at and an intellectual repose to talk to. Men who are dandies and women who are darlings rule the world, at least they should do so.' However, after he got to know Hughie better, he liked him quite as much for his bright buoyant spirits and his generous reckless nature, and had given him the permanent *entrée* to his studio.

When Hughie came in he found Trevor putting the finishing touches to a wonderful life-size picture of a beggar-man. The beggar himself was standing on a raised platform in a corner of the studio. He was a wizened old man, with a face like wrinkled parchment, and a most piteous expression. Over his shoulders was flung a coarse brown cloak, all tears and tatters; his thick boots were patched and cobbled, and with one hand he leant on a rough stick, while with the other he held out his battered hat for alms.

'What an amazing model!' whispered Hughie, as he shook hands with his friend.

'An amazing model?' shouted Trevor at the top of his voice; 'I should think so! Such beggars as he are not to be met with every day. A *trouvaille, mon cher**; a living Velasquez*! My stars! what an etching Rembrandt* would have made of him!'

'Poor old chap!' said Hughie, 'how miserable he looks! But I suppose, to you painters, his face is his fortune?'

'Certainly,' replied Trevor, 'you don't want a beggar to look happy, do you?'

'How much does a model get for sitting?' asked Hughie, as he found himself a comfortable seat on a divan.

'A shilling an hour.'

'And how much do you get for your picture, Alan?'

'Oh, for this I get two thousand!'

'Pounds?'

'Guineas. Painters, poets, and physicians always get guineas.'

'Well, I think the model should have a percentage,' cried Hughie, laughing; 'they work quite as hard as you do.'

'Nonsense, nonsense! Why, look at the trouble of laying on the paint alone, and standing all day long at one's easel! It's all very well, Hughie, for you to talk, but I assure you that there are moments when Art almost attains to the dignity of manual labour. But you mustn't chatter; I'm very busy. Smoke a cigarette, and keep quiet.'

After some time the servant came in, and told Trevor that the frame-maker wanted to speak to him.

'Don't run away, Hughie,' he said, as he went out, 'I will be back in a moment.'

The old beggar-man took advantage of Trevor's absence to rest for a moment on a wooden bench that was behind him. He looked so forlorn and wretched that Hughie could not help pitying him, and felt in his pockets to see what money he had. All he could find was a sovereign and some coppers. 'Poor old fellow,' he thought to himself, 'he wants it more than I do, but it means no hansoms for a fortnight;' and he walked across the studio and slipped the sovereign into the beggar's hand.

The old man started, and a faint smile flitted across his withered lips. 'Thank you, sir,' he said, 'thank you.'

Then Trevor arrived, and Hughie took his leave, blushing a little at what he had done. He spent the day with Laura, got a charming scolding for his extravagance, and had to walk home.

That night he strolled into the Palette Club about eleven o'clock, and found Trevor sitting by himself in the smoking-room drinking hock and seltzer.

'Well, Alan, did you get the picture finished all right?' he said, as he lit his cigarette.

'Finished and framed, my boy!' answered Trevor; 'and, by-the-bye, you have made a conquest. That old model you saw is quite devoted to you. I had to tell him all about you – who you are, where you live, what your income is, what prospects you have—'

'My dear Alan,' cried Hughie, 'I shall probably find him waiting for me when I go home. But of course you are only joking. Poor old wretch! I wish I could do something for him. I think it is dreadful that any one should be so miserable. I have got heaps of old clothes at home – do you think he would care for any of them? Why, his rags were falling to bits.'

'But he looks splendid in them,' said Trevor. 'I wouldn't paint him in a frock-coat for anything. What you call rags I call romance. What seems poverty to you is picturesqueness to me. However, I'll tell him of your offer.'

'Alan,' said Hughie seriously, 'you painters are a heartless lot.'

'An artist's heart is his head,' replied Trevor; 'and besides, our business is to realise the world as we see it, not to reform it as we know it. *A chacun son métier**. And now tell me how Laura is. The old model was quite interested in her.'

'You don't mean to say you talked to him about her?' said Hughie.

'Certainly I did. He knows all about the relentless colonel, the lovely Laura, and the £10,000.'

'You told that old beggar all my private affairs?' cried Hughie, looking very red and angry.

'My dear boy,' said Trevor, smiling, 'that old beggar, as you call him, is one of the richest men in Europe. He could buy all London tomorrow without overdrawing his account. He has a house in every capital, dines off gold plate, and can prevent Russia going to war when he chooses.'

'What on earth do you mean?' exclaimed Hughie.

'What I say,' said Trevor. 'The old man you saw today in the studio was Baron Hausberg. He is a great friend of mine, buys all my pictures and that sort of thing, and gave me a commission a month ago to paint him as a beggar. *Que voulez-vous? La fantaisie d'un millionnaire**! And I must say he made a magnificent figure in his rags, or perhaps I should say in my rags; they are an old suit I got in Spain.'

'Baron Hausberg!' cried Hughie. 'Good heavens! I gave him a sovereign!' and he sank into an armchair the picture of dismay.

'Gave him a sovereign!' shouted Trevor, and he burst into a roar of laughter. 'My dear boy, you'll never see it again. *Son affaire c'est l'argent des autres**.'

'I think you might have told me, Alan,' said Hughie sulkily, 'and not have let me make such a fool of myself.'

'Well, to begin with, Hughie,' said Trevor, 'it never entered my mind that you went about distributing alms in that reckless way. I can understand your kissing a pretty model, but your giving a sovereign to an ugly one – by Jove, no! Besides, the fact is that I really was not at home* today to any one; and when you came in I didn't know whether Hausberg would like his name mentioned.

You know he wasn't in full dress.'

'What a duffer he must think me!' said Hughie.

'Not at all. He was in the highest spirits after you left; kept chuckling to himself and rubbing his old wrinkled hands together. I couldn't make out why he was so interested to know all about you; but I see it all now. He'll invest your sovereign for you, Hughie, pay you the interest every six months, and have a capital story to tell after dinner.'

'I am an unlucky devil,' growled Hughie. 'The best thing I can do is to go to bed; and, my dear Alan, you mustn't tell any one. I shouldn't dare show my face in the Row*.'

'Nonsense! It reflects the highest credit on your philanthropic spirit, Hughie. And don't run away. Have another cigarette, and you can talk about Laura as much as you like.'

However, Hughie wouldn't stop, but walked home, feeling very unhappy, and leaving Alan Trevor in fits of laughter.

The next morning, as he was at breakfast, the servant brought him up a card on which was written, 'Monsieur Gustave Naudin, *de la part de** M. le Baron Hausberg.' 'I suppose he has come for an apology,' said Hughie to himself; and he told the servant to show the visitor up.

An old gentleman with gold spectacles and grey hair came into the room, and said, in a slight French accent, 'Have I the honour of addressing Monsieur Erskine?'

Hughie bowed.

'I have come from Baron Hausberg,' he continued. 'The Baron—'

'I beg, sir, that you will offer him my sincerest apologies,' stammered Hughie.

'The Baron,' said the old gentleman, with a smile, 'has commissioned me to bring you this letter;' and he extended a sealed envelope.

On the outside was written, 'A wedding present to Hugh Erskine and Laura Merton, from an old beggar,' and inside was a cheque for £10,000.

When they were married Alan Trevor was the best-man, and the Baron made a speech at the wedding-breakfast.

'Millionaire models,' remarked Alan, 'are rare enough; but, by Jove, model millionaires are rarer still!'

NOTES

Ruff's *Guide* and Bailey's *Magazine* (p123)
  two sporting journals, dealing with horse-racing and other sports –
  indispensable for a gentleman of this period
pekoe, souchong (p123)
  varieties of tea
bête (p124)
  (French) stupid
A *trouvaille, mon cher* (p125)
  (French) A find, my dear!
Velasquez (p125)
  Spanish realist painter (1599–1660), famous for his portraits
Rembrandt (p125)
  Dutch painter (1606–69), also celebrated for his portraits
A chacun son métier (p126)
  (French) Each to his own occupation
Que voulez-vous? La fantaisie d'un millionnaire! (p127)
  (French) What do you expect? The whim of a millionaire!
Son affaire c'est l'argent des autres. (p127)
  (French) Other people's money is his business.
not at home to any one (p127)
  not available or willing to receive visitors
the Row (p128)
  Rotten Row in Hyde Park, where fashionable Londoners went riding
de la part de (p128)
  (French) on behalf of

DISCUSSION

1 The first four sentences of the story set out what Wilde calls 'the great
   truths of modern life'. Yet Hughie defies them, and wins through
   regardless. Does this illustrate another great truth?

2 What kind of story is this? Is it just a light-hearted entertainment, or is
   there a moral in the story somewhere? If so, what might it be?

3 The Baron gets his painting; Alan gets paid; Hughie gets the £10,000
   he needs; Laura gets her husband. How many of these things are
   achieved honestly? Does it matter?

4   Suppose that the Baron gave Hughie, not £10,000, but a job in one of his banks. After saving for several years Hughie at last has enough money to marry Laura. How would this change the tone of the story? Would it change your response to the story, and if so, how?

LANGUAGE FOCUS

1   Wilde's memorable statements often work in pairs, for example: '*What you call rags, I call romance. What seems poverty to you is picturesqueness to me.*' What other instances of this can you find? How does this work? Is it more effective than a single statement?

2   Find these expressions in the text and explain them in your own words.

   * *Trevor was a painter. Indeed, few people escape that nowadays. But he was also an artist, and artists are rather rare.* (p124)
   * '*Men who are dandies and women who are darlings rule the world, at least they should do so.*' (p124)
   * '*There are moments when Art almost attains to the dignity of manual labour.*' (p125)
   * '*An artist's heart is his head, and besides, our business is to realise the world as we see it, not to reform it as we know it.*' (p126)
   * '*I can understand your kissing a pretty model, but your giving a sovereign to an ugly one – by Jove, no!*' (p127)

ACTIVITIES

1   Write the speech the Baron gave at the wedding breakfast, explaining how he came to know Hughie.

2   Write the conversation between the Baron and Alan after Hughie leaves, in which the Baron finds out about Hughie's circumstances.

3   Suppose Hughie comes to you today for some advice about his future. Write a report summarising his job history, his good and bad qualities, and your recommendations for a future career.

4   Is *The Model Millionaire* is a good title for this story? Do you think that Wilde chose it because it was a good pun rather than because it suits the story (which is more about Hughie than about the Baron)? What alternative titles, for example, *A Kind Heart Rewarded* or *A Gift Repaid*, do you think would be more appropriate or more interesting?

THE HERO

THE AUTHOR

Joanna Trollope was born in 1943 in Gloucestershire, and grew up in 'a very cold house with not quite enough food, but books were everywhere.' She studied at Oxford, worked in the Foreign Office and then taught while beginning to write for magazines. Success came first with historical novels, such as *Parson Harding's Daughter*, which won the Romantic Historical Novel of the Year award in 1980, *Charlotte*, and *The City of Gems*. Her first modern novel was *The Choir*, a highly successful exploration of life around a great English cathedral. Other bestsellers have followed – *The Rector's Wife, A Spanish Lover*, and *Marrying the Mistress* among them – and several of them have been televised. She writes perceptively about the frustrations of modern relationships, often in small communities where it is impossible to escape the scrutiny of others.

THE STORY

What an attractive idea it is – to be a writer. To take yourself away from everyday concerns and allow some great work to emerge from your brain into a new life of its own. And then to return to acclaim, fortune, celebrity . . . But where does the inspiration come from? How do you find that spellbinding story and release it into print?

'Writing calls on unused muscles and involves solitude and immobility,' said Dorothea Brande in her book *Becoming a Writer*. It requires much else too, of course, and the young man in this story finds that he has little to show for the hours he spends staring at his typewriter. How terrible if he has to return to the real world without a completed manuscript. Perhaps he needs to look outside himself. Perhaps there is a story waiting for him, out there, if only he can find it . . .

THE HERO

He stayed on the island much longer than he intended to. This was partly out of indolence and partly to prove all those people wrong – including his mother and his girlfriend – who had said that to decamp to a Mediterranean island for a whole winter to write a novel was both melodramatic and a cliché. He'd get sick of it in weeks, they said. He'd never write a book. He'd be lonely. Well, he *was* lonely in a way, and he was tired of the umbrella pines and the scrub-covered hills and the little port where the same old men sat outside the same old cafés and the same battered boats came in and out. But he had got used to it too, and to the slow rhythm of the days and in any case, his novel was only half done. When he thought about going home, his whole soul shrank from arriving back with only half a novel to show for seven months away with nothing else to do.

So he stayed. The winter – harsh and oddly bleak – wore away to the spring and he planted basil and geraniums on his tiny balcony and idled about in front of his typewriter. In the evenings, he went down to the harbour front and sat in one bar or another and read the local newspaper and joined in conversations about the weather or the fishing catch or the Mayor of the little port who had won on a Communist ticket, but who lived like a capitalist with a Mercedes and a villa with a swimming pool and a new wife who dressed like a harlot.

'It was different,' someone said one night, offering him one of the pungent local cigarettes, full of black tobacco, 'when we had the English Mayor. Quite different. He was a gentleman.'

He stopped lighting the cigarette and put it down.

'English? An English Mayor? Here?'

'Yes,' the old man said. He raised a hand. 'In 1944. I remember

him well. He was military governor.' He paused for emphasis. 'He
was a hero.'

Several other men nearby stopped talking and moved closer.

'It's true,' one said, 'my father knew him.'

'He's buried here,' the old man said. 'Didn't you know?'

He shook his head.

'I never heard of him—'

'You should have,' the old man said reprovingly. 'You an
Englishman and you don't know of Captain Campbell!'

'He's up the hill,' someone else said. 'There are six or seven
Protestants up there, in the cemetery beyond the water tower.
You'll find him there, with all his medals.'

'And when you've done that,' the old man said, stooping so that
he could peer directly into his face, 'you can go and see his widow.'

'His widow—'

'Yes, yes, his widow! Are you deaf? She is an islander, she lives
here, in the port, with her memories. She will tell you how it was
when Captain Campbell was the hero of this island!'

He woke next morning to a day of perfect spring, clear and blue
and polished. It was a Tuesday, the day on which the weekly letter
from his girlfriend usually lay waiting for him at the post office.
He decided, with a mixture of relief and guilt, that he was in no
hurry to collect it today, chiefly because, for the first time in
months, he had something other, and more pressing, to do. So he
draped a towel over his typewriter to smother its reproaches and
set off up the steep streets to the cemetery high above the port
where the Protestants had been safely segregated in death, away
from the Catholic faithful.

It was a tiny plot, surrounded by tumbledown walls and full of
tough winter weeds. There were half a dozen headstones, most at
crazy angles, but only one looked tended. The ground around it
had been roughly cleared and a red geranium had been planted in

a white plastic pot. The lettering on the stone was simple. 'Edward Archibald Campbell' it read, '1895–1957. D.S.O*. Croix de Guerre*.'

He looked at it for a long time and then at the earth under which Edward Campbell, husband, hero, and military governor, lay. Then, in a burst of sudden gratitude, he knelt for a moment, and closed his eyes. Below his knees lay not just a man, but a story.

∞

Signora Campbell was not at all surprised to see him.

'People come,' she said. 'People often come. To talk about my husband.'

Her villa was small and dark and crammed with furniture. It smelled of cats. Signora Campbell herself looked exactly like any other elderly islander, stout and dressed in black with grey hair held back in a bun with combs.

'But I was pretty once,' she said.

She showed him photographs of herself in 1944, proudly leaning against a tall, smiling man in uniform.

'That was Edward. He was very handsome.'

He said, 'Can you tell me about him?'

'He was a hero of the French Resistance,' she said, as if declaiming it. 'He helped British airmen who had baled out over occupied France to escape to England. The British gave him the D.S.O. The French,' she paused for dramatic effect, 'awarded him the Croix de Guerre.'

He peered about him in the gloom.

'Of course you have his medals—'

'No,' she said proudly. 'No. He was too modest to keep them. But I have this.'

She moved across the room and indicated a framed letter on the wall, a huge flamboyant, illuminated thing.

'From the people of the port,' she said, 'in grateful thanks. In humble thanks. Are you a journalist?'

'No,' he said, 'a writer.'

'Then to you I will entrust this.'

She went across the room to an ornate bureau and unlocked the topmost drawer. From it, she took a big, faded folder, tied up in pink lawyer's tape.

'His autobiography,' she said reverently. 'His own, true story. You must read it tonight and return it to me without fail tomorrow morning.'

He read all night. He couldn't stop. The style was crude and boyish but the story was spell-binding. Edward Campbell, youngest son of a small town Scottish doctor and educated by the Jesuits, had survived as a pilot with the Royal Flying Corps in the First World War. In the Second World War he had been recalled to buy transport in France for the British Expeditionary Force* in 1940 and, though overrun by the Germans, had eluded capture to become the vital organiser in the escape and evasion operation. After internment in Spain – on monstrously trumped-up charges – he had ended up as regional governor of the island, restoring order to a grateful civilian population after the chaos left behind by the retreating Axis*. He concluded the book in Somerset. 'I sit here to write the final page in the land I love, the land it has been my sole desire to serve.' It was *Boys' Own Paper** stuff and it was wonderful.

In the morning, he went back to Signora Campbell and begged to be allowed to borrow the manuscript for two weeks.

'Just a fortnight. I promise I'll return it. But there's someone I want to show it to. Someone in London. It's an amazing story.'

She made him sign a receipt with his English address as well as his address on the island. She was solemn when she shook his hand goodbye.

'You must be very trustworthy. You are taking my treasure.'

'Of course,' he said. He was much moved.

He kept the folder with him all the flight home, lying on his knees like a baby. Sometimes he would open it and take out a page, and the bold, smiling, nonchalant personality of Edward Campbell would rise up before him, as palpable as if he occupied the next airline seat. It was a story in a hundred thousand, a story to make not just a book but a film, an international film, with the final credits – including his own name as screenwriter – moving slowly over a last lingering shot of that simple, noble headstone among the weeds on a Mediterranean island.

∽

'Marvellous,' his agent said, 'a terrific story.'

He waited. His agent always reacted like this at first. It was the things he said next you had to listen to.

'A real boys' book. Plenty of action. Of course—'

'Yes?'

'We have to verify all this.'

'But I saw the grave . . .'

'Yes. But all the same. It won't be difficult, you know. He must be the star of half the books on the occupation of France and the French Embassy will know all about him. And the Ministry of Defence. Go and do a couple of days scouting about and I'll get this copied meanwhile. This could be a real spinner*, you know. It really could.'

∽

The assistant Military Attaché at the French Embassy was apologetic: 'You see, we have no record of Captain Campbell. But sometimes, in war the Croix de Guerre was awarded in the field* and never reached official records. Perhaps you could find more details from the British records? I am so sorry . . .'

The Army Records Office kept him waiting twenty minutes in a ferociously clean room painted shiny cream. He was conducted, at last, into an office where a man stood, half-smiling, behind a desk with his hand held out.

'Do excuse me for keeping you waiting. I was in a meeting, you see, but wanted to see you myself. Do sit down.'

He looked at the fat file on the man's desk. It seemed to contain, among other things, a manuscript.

'Captain Campbell, I believe. That's who you're after? I feel bound to tell you, I'm afraid, that you're not the first.'

He sat down abruptly, his eyes still fixed on the file.

'What do you mean?'

The man laid his hand on the file, almost affectionately.

'Terrific fellow. I've become quite fond of him over the years. But I'm afraid the whole thing's a fantasy. He was just a charming adventurer, with the gift of the gab—'

'But the honours!' he cried out. 'The D.S.O! The Croix de Guerre!'

'He invented them. He invented at least three-quarters of his life. It's an awful disappointment, I know. I felt it myself, when I first discovered. If it's any comfort to you, I've come to see that he believed it all himself in the end, every imaginary, boastful word of it.'

He went back to the island two days later, cradling the manuscript as carefully as he had done on the outward journey. He had felt in awe of it then; now he only felt protective, as if Edward Campbell must be shielded from the truth about himself as much as the island and the widow must be. He had no idea what he would say to the widow in actual words and phrases. All he knew was that he felt above all else that she must never know what he now knew. She and the island must keep their hero safe. It was his duty to make sure that they could.

He took a taxi from the airport straight to Signora Campbell's villa. She opened the door to him with an air of expectancy and, as if to add some mark of celebration, he saw she had added a string of amber beads to her stout black frock.

'Well?' she said.

He looked at her. Her eyes were bright. He was convulsed with the determination not to let her down.

He said slowly, to emphasise how much he was in earnest, 'I – decided it wasn't a story for the world. I'm so sorry. But it belongs here, you see. I've become convinced that it's a story for the island.'

'Quite so,' she said.

She reached out and almost snatched the folder from him, pressing it against her bosom. Her voice was exultant. 'Quite so.'

NOTES

D.S.O. (p135)
  Distinguished Service Order, a British medal awarded for bravery in war

Croix de Guerre (p135)
  French medal awarded for bravery in war

British Expeditionary Force (p136)
  part of the British Army which went to fight in France in the Second World War (1939–45)

Axis (p136)
  the alliance of the forces of Germany and Italy during the Second World War

Boys' Own Paper (p136)
  an early magazine for boys, characterized by inspiring stories of heroism and bravery

spinner (p137)
  (slang) a success

in the field (p137)
  on the battlefield

DISCUSSION

1 Seeing that the narrator wants to take over Captain Campbell's story as a substitute for producing his own, is he any less deceitful than Captain Campbell? What other similarities are there between the narrator and Captain Campbell?

2 Who is the most deceived in this story – the islanders? the widow? the narrator? Captain Campbell himself?

3 The man from the Army Records Office describes Captain Campbell as a 'terrific fellow', and his autobiography as a 'fantasy'. The locals on the island call him a 'gentleman'. Compare him with the present mayor, who is considered to be untrue to his principles. Is either morally superior to the other? How much of the respect shown to Captain Campbell is because of his character, do you think, and how much because of his imaginary exploits?

4 Why do you think the narrator decides not to reveal the deception at the end – and why have others done the same in the past?

5 Given the widow's reaction at the end of the story, how much do you think she knows of the truth about the autobiography? Is her reaction one of relief? Of triumph? From the way she reacts, what do you think might have happened before the narrator discovered Captain Campbell?

Language Focus

1 What lies behind these statements from the story? Explain their significance in the context of the story.

- *He draped a towel over his typewriter to smother its reproaches . . .* (p134)
- *Below his knees lay not just a man, but a story.* (p135)
- *You must read it tonight and return it to me without fail tomorrow morning.* (p136)
- *I was in a meeting, you see, but wanted to see you myself.* (p138)

2 This is a quiet, slow story, but actions often mark some significant shift in the situation. What changes are marked by these events?

- *He stopped lighting the cigarette and put it down.* (p133)
- *He knelt for a moment, and closed his eyes.* (p135)
- *She was solemn when she shook his hand goodbye.* (p136)
- *He sat down abruptly, his eyes still fixed on the file.* (p138)
- *She reached out and almost snatched the folder from him, pressing it against her bosom.* (p139)

Activities

1 Is *The Hero* a good title for this story? Why? Here are some alternative titles – are they better or worse, in your opinion?
The English Mayor   A Charming Adventure   Inventing the Past
What title would you give to the story?

2 Did you find the ending of the story satisfactory? What do you think will happen next? Suppose the agent begins to inquire about progress. How would the narrator explain the fact that he has not pursued his original plan? Write a paragraph to show how you think the story might continue, or, if you prefer, write a different ending altogether.

QUESTIONS FOR DISCUSSION OR WRITING

1 Of all the deceptions carried out in these different stories, which did
   you think was the most successful? Which was the most
   understandable, and which the most unpleasant? Who deceived for the
   best reasons, in your opinion, and who for the worst?

2 Which character did you sympathize with most in their deception?
   Which one had the most compelling reason to deceive, and which did
   you most hope would succeed?

3 Charles Churchill wrote:
       … wise fear, you know
       Forbids the robbing of a foe;
       But what, to serve our private ends,
       Forbids the cheating of our friends?
   Which stories involve the deception of someone close to the deceiver,
   and which involve deceiving a stranger, or someone to whom the
   deceiver does not feel any obligation? What difference does the
   intimacy of the relationship make to the deception?

4 The stories *Marionettes, Inc.*, *Telling Stories*, and *Mr Know-All* all
   involve a deception within a marriage. How are these marriages
   portrayed within the stories? Is the reader drawn to sympathize with
   the deceiver, or with the deceived? Is the deception helpful to the
   survival of the marriage, or does it simply draw attention to a fatal
   flaw within it?

5 In the stories *Taste* and *Mr Know-All* the knowledge of an expert is
   revealed – or appears to be revealed – as less reliable than we at first
   thought. Compare the way the two stories handle this revelation.
   Which is the more satisfying in your opinion?

6 Consider the central figures in the stories *The Coward* and *The Hero*. Both have a reputation that is based on deception, but only one of those reputations survives the events of the story. How and why do people react differently to Big Foot and the English Mayor? Do you find both stories convincing?

7 In two stories the deceptions are carried out by women, in two stories by men and women, and in the remaining six by men. What, if anything, do the deceivers of the same sex have in common? Are there any similarities in their motivation, for example, or in their circumstances? How do they differ from their counterparts of the opposite sex?

8 In *Sharp Practice* and *Neighbours* neither the judge nor the diplomat is able to confront his deceiver directly. Both are left to contemplate the deception after the event, and perhaps to reflect on how they contributed to it. Do you think their conclusions would be similar in any way? How do you think each man feels – resentful, amused, astonished, angry, resigned, irritated? What would they learn – about themselves, or about life – from the experience?

9 Which of the stories in this book did you like best, and why? Which would you recommend to a friend? Write a short review of the story for a newspaper or magazine.

10 Would any of the stories in this book make a good short film? Choose one, and write a description of the kind of film you would make. Would you take the viewpoint of the deceiver, or of another person in the story, or would you distance the telling of the story from the individuals concerned? Choose a key moment in your chosen story and write the screenplay for that scene, including directions for the actors.

THE EYE OF CHILDHOOD

Editors: John Escott & Jennifer Bassett

Short stories by

John Updike, Graham Greene, William Boyd,
Susan Hill, D. H. Lawrence, Saki, Penelope Lively,
Bernard MacLaverty, Frank Tuohy, Morley Callaghan

What does it feel like to be a child? Learning how to negotiate with the unpredictable adult world, learning how to pick a path through life's traps and hazards, learning when the time has come to put away childish things. The writers of these short stories show us the world as seen from the far side of the child–adult divide, a gap that is sometimes small, and sometimes an unbridgeable chasm.

AND ALL FOR LOVE . . .

Editors: Diane Mowat & Jennifer Bassett

Short stories by

Maeve Binchy, Edith Wharton, Virginia Woolf,
James Joyce, H. E. Bates, Graham Greene, Fay Weldon,
Patricia Highsmith, John Morrison, Somerset Maugham

What sad, appalling, and surprising things people do in the name of love, and for the sake of love. These short stories give us love won and love lost, love revenged, love thrown away, love in triumph, love in despair. It might be love between men and women, children and parents, even humans and cats; but whichever it is, love is a force to be reckoned with.